T0167051

SNOWDON'S DON
and
OTHER STORIES

SNOWDON'S DON
and
OTHER STORIES

Grace Moore

SNOWDON'S DON AND OTHER STORIES

Copyright © 2012 Grace Moore.

All rights reserved. No part of this book may be used or reproduced by any means, graphic, electronic, or mechanical, including photocopying, recording, taping or by any information storage retrieval system without the written permission of the author except in the case of brief quotations embodied in critical articles and reviews.

This is a work of fiction. All of the characters, names, incidents, organizations, and dialogue in this novel are either the products of the author's imagination or are used fictitiously.

iUniverse books may be ordered through booksellers or by contacting:

iUniverse
1663 Liberty Drive
Bloomington, IN 47403
www.iuniverse.com
1-800-Authors (1-800-288-4677)

Because of the dynamic nature of the Internet, any web addresses or links contained in this book may have changed since publication and may no longer be valid. The views expressed in this work are solely those of the author and do not necessarily reflect the views of the publisher, and the publisher hereby disclaims any responsibility for them.

Any people depicted in stock imagery provided by Getty Images are models, and such images are being used for illustrative purposes only.
Certain stock imagery © Getty Images.

ISBN: 978-1-4917-0631-2 (sc)
ISBN: 978-1-4917-0632-9 (e)

Library of Congress Control Number: 2019912168

Print information available on the last page.

iUniverse rev. date: 08/29/2019

Snowdon's Don

Jill had first known Ben from a writing group she attended infrequently. It met at the home of Marty Stevens and was composed of various young and promising anglophone Montreal writers, of whom Ben was one. These writers were all more promising and prolific than Jill, which was why she attended infrequently, being intimidated by the group.

Ben was the bad boy of the organization. He sat at the back of Marty's living room and made rude but witty remarks. His life style was less conventional than that of the others. It was rumored he had even been in prison.

Mostly she laughed at his jokes. Mostly she liked him. She was not overly interested. As her life got busier, she had no time for the writing group. She wanted to write at a more basic level.

She did not see Ben again for years. She heard that he had founded a theatre group. She saw his picture in the papers. He looked like a medieval Jewish prince, with long black ringlets.

All this passed her by. She never went to Ben's theatre. She went to Africa. When she came back, she settled in Notre-Dame-de-Grace in Montreal's west end. The area usually known as NDG, which spawned more community groups than all the rest of Montreal combined. Not the least of these was the Anti-Poverty Group, which had largely been brought up from neighboring Verdun by none other than Ben and a young Italian woman named Gina Petrelli. Gina actually administered most of the group's activities, while Ben was in charge of culture, and the founding of the Anti-Poverty Group's writing group.

Far from all this power and prestige, Jill first became a member of the Anti-Poverty Group when she saw an advertisement for it in a local laundromat. She started out answering the phones.

Ben made a point of visiting members of the NDG community, and especially of the Anti-Poverty Group, whom he thought might be interested in writing with an aim to establishing a writing group for poor people. Jill was not excluded. He came round to her place to talk to her, and she set aside her work to talk to him. "A writing group for poor people! What an excellent idea!" she exclaimed. "You have my total moral and artistic support."

"There are enough people in this community to make it feasible," he said, "I have only to visit a few more people, and I'm sure I'll be able to let you know when and where the first meeting will be."

He didn't stay long. She offered him coffee and cookies, but he refused. There were none of the nasty comments as in the old days. He was a man with a purpose, simply concerned about the task at hand. Jill was sure he would succeed. He was that good.

The first meeting of the Poor People's Writing Group was held at Head n' Hands, a local self-help group for youth. It was a small gathering of earnest souls. People read their half-finished poems and stories as Ben listened with extreme attention and professionalism, then gave advice to shape the work to come. He was patient. He was thoughtful. He was very, very good. When there was more general discussion, he participated in that as well.

"They have gotten themselves an excellent leader," Jill thought. She hadn't intended to fall in love with Ben. She had too much to do. But a deep loneliness inside her attracted her to him more than she realized. In him she recognized the quality of genius. She had known men who were conventionally bright, but not too many geniuses. After meetings of the writing group they would all sit around and Ben would regale them with his knowledge of history, religion - especially Judaism, philosophy, psychology, physics, almost any aspect of culture. He was a generalist, but one with more knowledge of most specific subjects than many specialists. He was revealed to Jill as an intellectual giant who devoted himself to the poor.

Jill was more than impressed. She was overwhelmed. Ben devoted the same expert attention to her writing as he did to everyone else's. "It's no good," she would say, "I'll never be a writer. I know what I want to say, but it comes out all wrong. It's cliché. It's melodramatic. It's all wrong. I'm no good."

"But you are good, "he would counter. "The woman you write about here shows your amazing insight into feminism. And last time your analysis was basically socialist. Your development of psychology is excellent. You are just so multi-faceted, if you would only see yourself for what you really are, instead of in terms of the stereotypes you have incorporated."

It was Jill who surpassed the boundaries in their relationship. Ben did not want her sexually, but she came to believe she had to have him. It began when she started writing little notes to him, in which she poured out her passion. At the same time she insisted on her insanity. "I love you, but only because I'm crazy" was the essence of what she said. Not very flattering for him.

He appeared to ignore the notes, and carried on as usual.

She could not sleep for thinking of him and one night at 2 AM she got up, got dressed and walked to his place. It was mid-winter and the snow was deep. He was still up, along with his male roommate, and they were reading, Ben in his bedroom and Wally, his roommate, at the kitchen table. Ben was flabbergasted by her visit. He tried to pawn her off on Wally, but she wasn't buying it. Instead, she came to his bedroom door. He got up to let her lie on his bed.

"What is it you want?" he asked, "street drugs or medication?"

She wanted neither of those two options. She wanted him. She stayed for a while, maybe an hour. Then she got up and trudged home.

Her next ploy was to invite him for supper. He would like that. Surprisingly, he accepted. She spent all day making special vegetarian dishes. He never showed up. She cried herself to sleep with enough food in the fridge for a week. As her involvement with Ben reached greater and greater levels of unreality, Jill's mental health deteriorated and the impossible happened. She lost her job with Green Energy on the basis of her inappropriate behavior. She had been with the organization for 8 years. She was drifting. She had less to do with her time.

Those in the Anti-Poverty Group also thought her behavior bizarre, but Gina would hear none of it. Jill stayed on there and the Group took up some of her now expanded time. There were more surprises in store.

The biggest one came when she arrived early at the writing group meeting one evening to find the male members of the group all discussing her as if she weren't there. "It's nothing less than sexual harassment that Jill has been guilty of practicing against me," Ben charged, "and I'm not going to put up with it any more. I need your support."

The other male members nodded gravely.

"They can't be serious," Jill thought.

They were deadly serious. "She should be thrown out of the group!" Phil cried.

"Let's put it to a vote."

So they voted, right in front of Jill, who was not asked to join them. All the male members voted for Jill's expulsion, but Jill did not vote against herself.

The next day she went to Gina, who said, "It's a lot of nonsense. Don't pay any attention to it. You're still in the group."

At this point, the writing group had its own office, which was under lock and key. Jill had been put in charge of the key, and the other members did not have a copy of it. At the next regular writing group time, she went to the office and opened it up for the meeting. Only a handful of people came, and they were all male members who had voted against Jill. Ben begged to have possession of the key, but Jill maintained a stony silence. After about half an hour the male members all left. Jill stayed until the regular time for the group to finish, then locked up and went home. The next week, Ben came alone to confront Jill, and to beg again for the key. She responded with the same stony silence until he gave up and left.

For the third time since her "ousting", Jill came and opened the office for the group. This time no one came. Jill sat there for the whole three hours allotted to the meeting, then locked up and went home. The next day she handed the key over to Gina, announcing "The Poor People's Writing Group has folded."

Even her attempted ousting and the demise of the group could not, however, eradicate the powerful influence of Ben on Jill's mind. She never saw him again after the folding of the group, but she did not lose the ability to fantasize.

She thought about Ben's poverty. Oh they all were poor, but Ben was poorer than the average community worker. She had noticed that on her visit to his apartment at 2AM. Ragged furniture, few appliances, junk food in the cupboard. Had he actually been in prison? What had happened with his theatre group?

But she knew, it was well documented, that somehow, somewhere, he had done time in Bordeaux jail. She had no idea what for. Somewhere, maybe only in her own mind, she had heard conflicting stories. Confused, conflicting stories. People didn't want to talk about it. One story was that he had been found guilty of criminal negligence in the death of a little Verdun girl. One story said he was not actually guilty of this offence, merely found guilty because of anti-semitism.

They said he went to Bordeaux a scared little boy, who would not have survived there had he not been protected by the mob, who taught him to shoot and hit a moving target using their stock in trade, a 45 caliber handgun. How they managed all of this from prison Jill did not know, but she believed it was possible.

When Ben was released after having served his time, he was a full fledged mafia hit-man, but he did not keep a gun at home. Rather he borrowed one from the local police station for emergencies. He became active in the political underground and, because he was originally from the Snowdon area, he became known as Snowdon's don.

The story was barely plausible, but Jill believed it implicitly. In reality, all she knew was that Ben had been in Bordeaux. There may actually have been a connection between that and the earlier downfall of Ben's theatre group, whether or not there was any little Verdun girl involved.

With plenty of time on her hands, Jill started to frequent what was perhaps the most well known of all NDG night clubs, Maz, on Sherbrooke St. West. She went alone, and mainly to dance. She did not drink much. She danced alone, and often so lewdly she was asked to leave. But she kept coming back, promising good behavior, because she heard Ben's voice in the behind the scenes operations of the night club where, with his cronies, he exercised power as "Commander Ben and equipe." She was in complete solidarity with him.

She believed there was an organization of wrong-assed local feminists who were out to get her because of her involvement with Ben (through the wires). When she had a massive menstrual hemorrhage one evening she blamed it on this group.

She did not go to a doctor. Instead, she made up a little, magical, refrain,

"Blood bath of holy Zion, Ben
What d'ye do this time, Ben?
And as to the encore
A la gauche, Ben."

In the midst of a winter snowstorm, believing she was being persecuted in her NDG apartment, she trudged to her friend Vicki's place below the tracks, to pay an unannounced visit. "C'mon in!" said Vicki, surprised, "What are you doing out on a night like this?"

"I'll only stay a little while, "said Jill. "I just couldn't stand it in my place any more.'

"You can curl up there on the sofa for as long as you want. I'm going to bed myself."

Jill took the sofa, and slowly began to sob herself to sleep as Ben's woman.

She heard Ben's voice in her head on many, many other occasions. She was almost constantly in touch with him that way. He proposed to her, through the wires. Wires of her own imagination, she thought, but she did not know that. In her imagination, they became engaged. They would get married in a synagogue and have the reception at Maz.

Jill went to Ota jewelers and bought herself a gold wedding band for $65.She knew other single women who wore wedding rings so as to avoid the unwanted attentions of certain men. Jill wore hers just to imagine she was married, not all the time, only when she most felt like identifying as Ben's wife.

She decided she needed a cat, who would represent Ben to her in her home. There were black cats and white cats, but no Jewish cats. Through the wires, Ben told her "The closest thing to it is a Persian."

She found an ad in the paper advertising Persian kittens for sale and went to a home in Chomedey, where she purchased one for $250. It was much more than she could afford, but it was worth it, for Ben. It was a playful little thing and she enjoyed its company for a few weeks. She named it Kin-ig, after the two words from which the English word king is derived. She had discovered this doing research on the subject in university. The words meant "spirit of all the people."

One evening, when she was again feeling persecuted, this time because she felt racial tensions in NDG, she put Kin-ig in a cloth bag and walked to

Verdun. There she went into a variety of bars and restaurants before ending up in a kind of fast food hamburger joint which was open all night. Mostly teen-agers hung out there. For some reason, the staff would not serve her. She did not protest, but started to sing and dance quite loudly, attracting considerable attention. Finally, when she was exhausted, she sat at a booth with a number of teen-agers. They gave her some leftover French fries with cigarette ashes in them. Otherwise, they seemed friendly. She decided to take Kin-ig out of the bag. Then they freaked.

"On va manger le chaton! On va vraiment le manger!" they cried.

"Do they really mean that?" Jill asked herself. "They want to eat Kin-ig?"

She panicked She decided it was time to leave. Quickly, she put Kin-ig back in the bag and left. The teen-agers followed her outside, where they attacked her. But they were only kids, and she fought them off.

It was 3 o'clock in the morning, but she started walking back to NDG. She got about half a kilometer down the road when a big transport truck, with 2 burly men in it, pulled up. The man on the passenger side got out and grabbed the bag with Kin-ig in it.

Then he got back in the truck and the two men drove off

It was sad. Jill felt both defeated and humiliated. She trudged back to NDG alone. By the time she got there it was daylight.

She didn't want to blame Verdun too much. Perhaps it had its own reasons for wanting Kin-ig. But Kin-ig was hers, and perhaps also Ben's. He symbolized Ben and the symbolization was broken with his capture in Verdun. Verdun didn't know that, but perhaps now Kin-ig symbolized Ben's spirit in Verdun.

They came and took Jill away and put her in a psychiatric hospital. The police and the ambulance came. She never knew who sent them.

In the hospital, they gave her medication and forced her to confront their version of reality. She came to know that she was not engaged to Ben, had never been. She would never marry him. She found out that he had left NDG. She did not find out where he had gone. In time, over the years, as she got on with her life, she realized she no longer cared where he was or what he did.

Money Back

Stranded in the ghetto after Cleveland, and living in a rooming house again, her room was so small she could barely fit her few belongings into it. There was a bed, a hotplate and a bureau, but no place for her suitcases or boxes of books, which she would have to abandon. She kept her precious thesis, however, hoping she would find a way to work on it again some day. The room made her claustrophobic. She could not be expected to stay there. So she hung around at the McGill Student Union, both to have more space, and to find out what was going on.

At the McGill Student Union she met up with the Trotskyists, or more specifically one of their splinter organizations, the Groupe Marxiste Revolutionaire. Commonly known as the GMR, it saw itself as the vanguard of the 4th International and did not respond well to accusations of splintering on the part of the mainstream Trots. "It's just that our positions really are more advanced", they explained. To Jane, it was all new. She had not been acquainted with the Trotskyist movement at all before. To her, Leon Trotsky had been just a figure in history. Certain aspects of Marxism attracted her, particularly Marx's early writings on alienation, which she found compatible with the works of her hero, Jean-Paul Sartre.

Now, she began to see in Trotsky's works and in some of the writings about him, a continuation of the same intellectual tradition. She didn't much go in for the partisanship, the factions on the left, but she came to believe that Trotsky had been the best thing happening in Soviet Russia at his time. She hung around with the GMR because they were more prominent on campus than other groups. She believed in them, and then she met Gérard. A short, slight, wiry little man, with a red beard and a mane of thick red hair which fell well beneath his shoulders. He was accompanied by a big red dog, whom he introduced as "Cayenne", and who had a coat of hair the exact same color as his own.

"Did you get him to match your hair?" Jane asked.

" No, it's purely coincidental. He's a great dog. Very affectionate and easy to train. Part collie. I got him because I fell in love with him. Of course, I could have dyed my hair to match him, but I didn't have to."

A staunch member of the GMR, Gérard hung around with Jane at the Student Union. One night he asked her, "How would you like it if I took you home? I'd love to show you my place."

He lived on Rivard Street, in the extreme east end of the McGill student ghetto, the francophone section. Jane found his flat comfortable and much more spacious than her room. He had decorated it sparsely, mostly with posters of left wing events and heroes. A concert by Edith Piaf. The inevitable poster of Che. Gérard lived alone, except for Cayenne. Jane was intrigued, and impressed. She did not stay long. As she left, he said to her, "Come back sometime." He looked lonely. As if a dog, no matter how affectionate, didn't always provide enough company. Looking at the paint beginning to peel on his walls, he added, thinking this necessary for a woman, "I'm going to fix the place up."

Jane did go back, several times. She liked him. And inevitably, they made love. Right there on the floor of his place, which he had not in the least fixed up. She found him a good lover, spontaneous and uninhibited. Capable of both enjoying himself and giving her pleasure as well.

When he saw where she actually lived, he was very upset. "No. You can't stay here. You will live with me. I have lots of space."

So she loaded up her scanty belongings, including her thesis, and moved in with him. It was a big improvement. He insisted on sharing the housework. "I have done it for so long you will have difficulty doing it to please me anyway." Jane didn't mind for the most part, but she liked to cook. Only very occasionally would he let her do this for him. "You English don't cook well," he declared. "I must do it my own way."

They went out frequently, to political meetings but also to have a good time. Like most young people, they loved to dance. They went to clubs and danced until the early hours of the morning. They tumbled off the walls as well as the floors.

They went to parties in the homes of other GMR members, where they frequently made love on the floor or in the open. No one cared. No one noticed.

Jane decided she wanted to be a Trotskyist. She read all the literature, including the books by Trotsky himself. But when she mentioned this to Gérard, he laughed. "You a Trotskyist? You a member of the 4th Internationale? No, no, no, you may read somewhat but you cannot claim to be an intellectual. You may be my girlfriend, but you do not need to know all the revolutionary literature. Is that not enough for you?"

The other members of the GMR saw it the same way. Jane could have a good time, but she was not to be taken seriously. Jane thought about her uncompleted thesis in ritual drama, but wondered whether she should bring it up now.

A little while later he proposed. "You will marry me?" He made it part question, part command. She could think of no other answer than "Yes". After all, the sex was good.

To get a marriage certificate you had to have a birth certificate. Gérard showed Jane his. It said that Gérard Lévesque was the son of Réne Lévesque. "Oh," gasped Jane, "not the former premier!"

"This certificate," said Gérard, studying her, "is useful for political purposes, It is useful to have Gérard Lévesque, the Trotskyist, lined up under Réne Lévesque, the Péqiste and former premier. That is all most people notice. They don't ask questions. But, if we get married, I'm afraid they might ask too many questions. Besides, I was brought up a Catholic and if we get married in the Catholic church, you would have to convert. Are you interested in that?"

"No."

"Then what church were you brought up in?"

"The United Church of Canada."

"Then we'll get married there."

Next day, Jane went down to St. James United Church on Ste. Catherine St., and made inquiries about a marriage certificate. "Here's my birth certificate," she said to the clerk, who glanced at it briefly and set it aside "and this one is my boyfriend's." As Jane had expected, the clerk hesitated somewhat over Gérard's birth certificate, before finally accepting it. Carefully, she filled out the marriage certificate.

"That will cost you $15."

Jane paid the nominal amount out of her own pocket. She left the church and went into a dry goods store, where she found the clerk from the church following her from a discrete distance.

Shortly after this, Gérard and Jane went out one evening to a friend's place. They made love on the floor as usual. He penetrated her long and deep and Jill later found out, as she had suspected, that she was pregnant. It didn't matter. They had promised each other they would get married. But she didn't tell Gérard she was pregnant.

Things began to go wrong in the household. Jane was disappointed and insulted at not being a Trot. Not being a full-fledged member of the GMR. Also, the good sex did not compensate for a lot of other things. Gérard's behavior became more and more domineering. Whereas he used to allow Jane some choice in their diet, he now decided what they would eat without consulting her. When she shopped he told her what to buy. He began to tell her who to associate with and what to say to them. When they went out together he decided what she would wear. He seemed afraid she might embarrass him. She became horribly aware that he had found her in a rooming house.

Jane got out her thesis, but she knew it wouldn't help with Gérard. Its topic didn't interest him. "Bourgeois," he claimed. "It's nothing but bourgeois research."

"At least it's historical, "she said, but he was only interested in intellectuals he could clearly distinguish as being on the left. He was interested in a different kind of intellectual than she was. Or in no intellectual at all. As far as she became aware, his ideal intellectuals might well have been mythical.

His constant authority developed unbearable proportions. They fought. One night, as she turned away from him in bed, she said, "I do not think we will get married."

He answered, "Obviously, we will not get married."

Jane went down to the church and got her money back.

She moved out, without Gérard's ever knowing she was pregnant. She went to a community clinic. "You're pregnant," they told her. "Why didn't you come to us about birth control?"

"But it wasn't like that. It's not as if we were irresponsible. We planned to get married."

"And now you're not going to?"

"There's been a change in plans."

"Well, I suppose we'll have to try to get you an abortion somewhere, if that's what you want."''

''It is."

In a couple of days they called. "Your abortion is scheduled for the Montreal General Hospital two weeks from Tuesday".

When she showed up for the abortion they informed her, "There is a legal requirement that you give the reason for your wanting the abortion."

She wrote "Neither my boyfriend nor I are psychologically or financially capable of supporting a child at this time." The reason was accepted.

She was too late for a D&C and had to have the saline method. The abortion went smoothly. She had no difficulty expelling the tiny fetus and as it plopped into the pan she thought, ""If this were all there were to having children, I might still have some one day."

But she knew there was a lot more to it than that.

There's Your Blood

She was 21, and her virginity hung heavily upon her. She wanted to get rid of it, and she would do so as soon as she found an appropriate partner.

In the past, she had gotten into trouble because of her virginity. All around her, people were losing theirs and she was not. It wasn't just that they were losing their virginity, they were also not doing other things they should be doing, like working or studying, and Mona had to complain about that. She gained a reputation for keeping her virginity, but that was not the point. The point was studies, at which she wanted to succeed more than sex.

That was all behind her now. That had been in Newfoundland. Now was Montreal. She had her own apartment and she was working, not studying. She was free. It was just a matter of finding the right man. She had never thought she would find him on the street. She had expected more ceremony. But on the street was where she did find him.

She was walking toward her brother's place in the McGill student ghetto one day, when she happened to notice a handsome olive skinned man with high cheekbones and jet black hair. He was small and slim and he was obviously looking at her. When she knew that he had caught her eye, he approached.

"I see you walking here from my window every day. I live just around the corner over there. My name is Anwar. And you are?"

"Mona. My brother lives right across from you. It's him I come to see. I'm new here, so he has to help me out."

"Where are you from?"

"Newfoundland."

"Oh, Newfoundland. I'm Pakistani. You must have heard all about the Newfoundlanders and Pakistanis in Toronto."

"They say they're the 2 most colorful groups there."

"Perhaps we could start our own community here."

"2 people hardly make a community. What do you do?"

"I'm a student in economics at McGill. I would like to get to know you a bit better, miss. Why don't we go have coffee at the McGill Sandwich Shop over there?"

"Well, my brother is expecting me, but perhaps we could go later, around seven?"

"OK. I'll be waiting for you in the restaurant."

After her visit with her brother was through, she went to find Anwar in the restaurant, where they had coffee and chatted. He had been in Montreal for 2 years, she for 2 months. He was a bit lonely, but independent. She was still fascinated with the bright lights of the city.

After they had finished their coffee, and she got up to leave, he asked if he could walk her to her place. When they got there he wanted to come in. Since he was so handsome and so friendly, she decided she wouldn't refuse him.

Soon they were kissing, mouth to mouth. He was a passionate kisser. He began to undo the buttons of her blouse.

She withdrew. "There's something I should tell you, "she said. "I've never done this before. Not that I don't want to, you understand, but you'll have to be patient with me."

"Well," he laughed, "I've done it hundreds of times before, so don't worry. If we don't go the whole way tonight, we'll do it some other time," He pulled her closer.

They got all their clothes off, and she squealed with delight as he massaged her breasts. Then he massaged the rest of her body, expertly, deliberately, before he gently parted her legs and began to enter her. She was tight. She was a real virgin. He gave up and said, "It doesn't matter. I'll come back tomorrow night."

He came back the next night and the next night and the night after, and each time he entered her he went a little further. She began looking for blood on the sheets, for some proof that her hymen had been broken.

His entries were painless, so painless and gradual that when he finally went the whole way she did not know that that was what had happened. He pointed to the sheets and said, "There's your blood!"

After that, they saw each other less often. She wanted him, but he would not be committed. She didn't try to force him. That was not part of their unspoken deal.

He gave her a few presents - a small Dutch lamp, a book of cartoons from the New Yorker, pralines.

Soon, he faded out of her life. She had only a twinge of regret. She was glad that she had fulfilled her ambition to lose her virginity. She felt strangely mature.

Possibly Exiting Gabon

He came over to Gabon while she was there. He was a WUSC official whose job it was to investigate her situation as well as those of the other WUSC volunteers in Gabon.

They met in the only restaurant in downtown Oyem. She was attracted to him, but it did not look good. They were saying she did not know French, that she had to get out of Gabon. It was all lies, of course, like the other information that had come through the mail from the WUSC office, insisting she pay back student loans when it had been agreed she wasn't to do that until her contract was up.

They sipped on pina coladas and coconut milk and ate brochettes of very European beef and local, tender, fish.

"Why did you come here in the first place?" he wanted to know. "I suppose it's better than being a waitress?"

She said nothing. Nothing about her degrees, her true reasons for coming.

"Well," he continued when he saw she wasn't going to answer, "you may be able to stay in Africa, but you'll have to go to an anglophone country."

"Look," she insisted, "Marilyn MacLeod is with the Peace Corps. Her French is far worse than mine, but nobody complains about her."

"Head office isn't satisfied. Do you disagree with that?"

"All of a sudden head office isn't satisfied. I'm an anglophone. My French isn't perfect, but it was good enough up until about a month ago, when I also started getting illegitimate complaints about student loans. I don't like it. Something fishy is going on They're trying to force me out of here, against my contract."

"All I can do is implement whatever head office tells me to do, and your future in Gabon does not look rosy. Oh look," he continued, suddenly contrite, "I'm not saying it's all your fault. Anyway, the decision won't be made right away. You can count on enjoying yourself here for another month or 2 at least. Now tell me about yourself. How did a Newfoundlander get mixed up in this exotic country anyway?"

She ignored the snub. Soon she was telling him her life history, or at least the parts of it she felt it was safe for him to hear. He was from Quebec, francophone but perfectly bilingual. He ordered another round of pina coladas and said,

"Would you like to dance?"

He steered her onto the postage stamp restaurant dance floor.

At the end of the set, there were more pina coladas, and more still at each break from the dancing after that. Each time she got up to dance her dancing became more erratic. He held her, to steady her at first.

"C'mon," he said eventually," this place closes in 15 minutes. Come back to the hotel with me."

The hotel, the only one in town, was a huge white elephant which housed visiting dignitaries and whoever else it could find.

They walked across the thick grass wet from the recent rain and up a narrow red path to the sumptuous hotel doors. Inside the modern elevator, he steadied her again 'til they reached the 4th floor and he found his room. It was dark and cozy with only a dim white light around the baseboard, a chest of drawers and a waterbed. They fell on the bed together and he held her again, this time with a little more urgency. She turned toward him. He was a handsome man, and she was in every way intoxicated, with the pina coladas as much as she was with him. She let him undress her. She helped him undress himself. Everything was quiet now, peaceful. She liked that. She liked the quiet in him. "I'm married," he told her, as if it were something he thought she should know. They knew it wouldn't make a difference between them. She was only aware of his experience in bed. He made love to her slowly, perfectly, caressing her breasts, then stroking the soft hair between her legs, which he patiently opened so that he could enter her. She responded to him with serenity. After he had come, she realized she was so drunk she did not know whether she had or not. They slept then, and when they awoke she asked,

"How can I contact you in Montreal?"

"No, you can't do that, "he answered.

"Because you're married?"

"Yes."

She got dressed then and walked the 8 miles from Oyem to the village of Angone, where she lived. It was morning, but the heat was already strong and the road was a blazing red.

As she neared the school compound where she worked in Angone, she saw Frère Fernand coming around the corner of the Brothers' residence. She waved to him and smiled, but somehow she couldn't help thinking that he knew all about her terrible night of sin, and about how she was being forced to ponder her future.

The Wrestler

They met at some left-wing gathering in the McGill student ghetto, in what used to be known as the University Settlement building. He was short, somewhat overweight, and not at all physically attractive. But that didn't stop them from being friends. There was something about him she liked, even respected. He was a graduate in history from Concordia University, and from his speech it was clear that he knew his stuff. He was not working at present, however, and he felt somewhat guilty and uncomfortable about that. Jill's heart went out to him. She was sure he would find something soon. He should not give up. But he still felt inferior to the other leftists, whom he saw as much more productive than himself. He felt he was not pulling his weight in saving the world.

"Look at me," said Christine, "I'm still struggling after an MA in English. And it took me long enough to do that. It doesn't come easy. Right now, I'm doing some ESL work for a private language school, and I hate it. I find it very stressful. I want to be a college instructor eventually."

"Yes, well, I will keep trying. But you know, I didn't get very good grades for my BA. I know my history because I like history and I read off the course list a lot. My father also taught me a good bit of what I know. But these other radicals! I try as best I can. I work really hard in the movement but they don't respect me. They don't take me seriously. I tell you, you almost have to have a PhD to get anywhere today, on the left as much as anywhere else."

They left the meeting. "Would you care to come to a restaurant for coffee? Not an expensive one. I can't afford that."

"We could always go to the McGill Sandwich Shop. It's not too far away."

It was about a 10 minute walk. When they got there, they ordered coffee and started talking about more ordinary things, such as domestic arrangements."

"I'm not satisfied with my place," she said. "It's very small and far too expensive."

"I'm living with my parents in Snowdon for the moment, but I have some friends who operate a coop on Ste. Famille St. It's not expensive and I'm going to move in there at the beginning of the month. I think they have another room available. I could inquire for you if you like."

"Would you? I can't say definitely that I'll go there. I'd need to know more about it, and I'll have to think about it, but it sounds interesting."

He gave her some details. It was a small coop, run by John and June, a married couple with 2 young boys. There was no cumbersome committee, no by-laws. Everyone pitched in with the work. The housework was managed by June. John mostly did the accounts. Everyone had their own small room, but complete run of the rest of the house. And the rent was a fraction of Christine's current one. John and June were basically hippies. They didn't care much about money, but they did like to have their friends around them.

Christine went with Alex to meet John and June. She found them charming and friendly. Everything seemed perfect. She gave them a deposit of a month's rent and arranged to move out of her old, expensive place.

Mostly, it was fun living in the coop. John and June were pleasant, easy-going relaxed. The boys, Jacob, aged 8, and Timmy, aged 4, were angelic models of good behavior, for the most part. When they did err briefly, they were all the more adorable for that. There were no problems with the eating or the cleaning, no strict rules about when or when not to play music, as long as it wasn't too loud. Christine could live with the "house rules". What she was having difficulty living with was Alex.

They had separate rooms. It shouldn't have been that difficult. They were friends. They should have been free to go their own separate ways, within the coop as outside. So Christine thought.

Alex didn't see it that way. As he had gotten Christine into the coop, he believed this was tantamount to her agreeing to be his sexual partner. He devised ways of getting her into his room.

At first she didn't mind. Then one evening she even consented to have sex with him. It was a disaster. It wasn't a question of whether or not he was attractive to her. It was just that he was no good at it, not in the least! And there were reasons for this. It was obvious to her that all his views on sexuality were based on pornography. When he touched her he did not touch her, but something else, a product of his own imagination. She could not respond to him anymore than he could respond to her. He did not see her as a live being. She knew the meaning of the term "sex object". She had never felt so objectified in all her life!.

She didn't know how to tell him all this. That his problem was basically porn. So she tried to tell him, "Look, if you see me for real, if you respond to my body and not to your imagination, we might get somewhere."

But he did not listen. To him, the problem was all hers.

"You bitch! I got you into this coop. Now you turn out to be a fair weather friend. When I want you, you're not there for me."

"But that's not it. This is an impossible situation. Listen to me. I've had a lot of sex, and I bet you haven't had any except for your porn magazines. I could teach you, if you want, but you don't seem to be listening."

"Ah, go to hell. I've also been to a few whores, you know."

He grabbed her, and she sighed and resigned herself to the non-communication. She did not give in completely, it was just a lot easier to deal with him if she didn't provoke him too much.

All the while she stayed there, he kept up the same frustrating game. To control her sexually, he would often get her into wrestling strangleholds, which, had she not been agile enough to wriggle out of them, would have suffocated her. He didn't believe there was any danger. He didn't know his own strength.

She threatened to call the police, but he said he'd get back at her if she did that, because of his politics.

For that reason, she decided to move out of the coop. John and June, even the kids, were sorry to see her go. They had liked her. But she felt that as Alex had been the one to know the coop, to know John and June first, he should be the one to stay, and she would find another place.

She did find one that was acceptable and not too expensive. Nothing could replace the coop of course, but it would do. It was actually not too far from the coop.

This was fine until she found Alex on a street corner one block away from her new place one day. He proceeded to attack her physically, hitting and scratching. She managed to get away without serious harm. Then, another day, the same thing happened on another street corner. It got to be he was always there waiting for her, on some street corner near her place. Obviously he had at least a vague idea of where she lived.

Then suddenly, he stopped. Instead he called her. He apologized for his aggressive behavior and wanted to be friends again. He was going to see a psychiatrist.

He did not meet her on the street again after that, did not beat her up again. But he did call her a few more times, did let her know about how his psychiatric treatment was going.

Christine couldn't help but be skeptical. She sympathized with him about the psychiatry, but would psychiatry cure pornography? Could it? It was a social, not an individual, disease. Psychiatry couldn't even cure the major neuroses and psychoses, and was pornography one of these?

She was going away for the Christmas holidays. She said good-bye to Alex and said she would talk to him when she got back.

When she got back from the holidays, she got a call from John.

"Alex is dead."

"Oh, I'm truly sorry to hear that."

She was shocked and amazed. She realized how much she had actually liked the guy, felt sympathy for him in spite of his anti-social behavior.

He died of an embolism of the lung, perhaps related to his being overweight. Christine went to his funeral with John and June and grieved along with the others. Some of his other friends didn't seem to think she should have been there. Some even blamed her, strangely, for his death. She knew she had treated him as well as she could.

Fag Hag

In the winter of 1976, Joan was studying towards a PhD. in Études anglaises at the Université de Montréal. She moved into a small apartment on de Bullion Street, in the east end of the McGill student ghetto. She had just been released from the Allen Memorial psychiatric institute, and she was feeling somewhat depressed. She had moved to the apartment to get away from her former room-mate, Nancy Watson, who was extremely congenial, but, in her depressed state, Joan just could not live up to her mirth She wanted to be alone to think, or even to brood, in private.

As she was moving her things up the narrow winding staircase to the 3rd floor – not a small feat as she had two broad armchairs and a table – she was greeted enthusiastically by a man in the corridor of the second floor below. His enthusiasm reminded her of Nancy, but she turned anyway. He looked about thirtyish, was of medium height and build and had a distinguishing shock of short blond hair which had a habit of falling over his forehead, and which he was constantly pushing back. He had an attractive, boyish, pointed face with a prominent, distinguished nose.

"Hello," he said. "Moving in, I see. My name is Corey.

Corey King, Apartment 29. You must come and have coffee with me. No, come for a meal. I'm an excellent cook, and I like to organize the building, unofficially."

"And why do you think I need organization?"

He shrugged his shoulders. "Everybody does."

Joan was taken aback by his boldness, but she felt she should show appreciation for his offer, much as she had hoped to be left alone. "Well," she said, "I'm busy right now with the moving, but if you'll invite me for 7, I should have everything taken care of by then."

"See you at 7 then. Oh, by the way, I'm from Nova Scotia. I'm going to make you clam chowder, plus a salad with shrimp. Hope you like seafood."

"Really! I'm from Newfoundland myself."

"Same thing."

"No, it isn't. It isn't at all."

Joan finished her unpacking a bit hurriedly and was ready in plenty of time for her dinner engagement. There was something about this obviously extroverted man that had the power to elate her, as Nancy could not. Why was he so busy organizing everybody? If you could believe what he said.

When 7 PM came, she timidly knocked on the door of #29. He opened it with a flamboyant bow. He showed her into the tiny living room, which was jam-packed with artifacts and knickknacks, but everything was clean and neatly organized. Corey led her to a decoratively set table and said, "Food's ready. It'll be here in a minute."

He went to the miniature kitchen and brought out first the clam chowder, then a garden salad with mushrooms.

"I love mushrooms," Joan said.

There was also a huge shrimp casserole, baguettes and butter, and a cool bottle of white wine.

"Now, my dear," he said, "we're all sot."

"Hey, that's a Newfoundland expression!"

"Well, my mom's a Newf, but I was brought up in Cape Breton,.
Best scenery in the world."

"If not second to Newfoundland, The Rock."

"I won't argue. I've been to The Rock a few times. But to me home is Cape Breton. I find it a little less isolated and more convenient."

"Been in Montreal long?"

"For years now, but I still go home every summer. How about you?"

"Whenever I get the chance. Whenever I have the money."

"You a student?"

"Yeah, how did you know?"

"No money."

"Well what do you do?"

"I'm a teacher. I teach English in a little private French school. Been doing it for 6 years now, so there's some security. I have a BA in English."

"Interesting. I'm doing a PhD. in Études anglaises at the Université de Montréal. It's actually an English lit. program except for a couple of courses in Québecois literature you have to do in French. What did you mean when you said you were organizing the building? Anything special?"

"Yes, actually. You see, I'm gay. And there are a lot of other gays in the building. I try to keep an eye on them and make sure no one gets into trouble. Oh, I'm quite sociable with heterosexuals as well, as long as they're not prejudiced. How about you? You're not gay by any chance, are you? You're not prejudiced?"

"I'm not gay. I'm not prejudiced."

"Then I'll introduce you to the gang. There's Sheila in 37 and Gail in 22 Gail's brother is a bigwig in City politics. Sheila and Gail used to be lovers, but they've split up now and Gail has a new girlfriend. She doesn't live in the building. Then there's Denis in 40 and Roy in 42. They're lovers. Oh, let me show you something. C'mon, don't be scared. "He led her to the bathroom door, which was notched from bottom to top.

"There's a notch for every man I've brought home to this apartment." Joan's face fell. "You slept with all these men?"

"Not with all of them. Some I just invited for supper, but most of them I've slept with, yes." He beamed. "Actually, my permanent partner is in Boston. I see him every second week-end. I am the world's poorest member of the jet set. When Sam's not around, I am free to see whomever I choose. I do take precautions, in case you're wondering. I know how to look after myself."

"What's he like, your lover in Boston?"

"He's a bit older than me. Jewish. Almost blind. He's a businessman. I'll bring you down to meet him sometime."

"Oh, that won't be necessary."

" Seriously. He's a nice guy. He'd be happy to meet you."

When Joan went back to her apartment she found that her usual depression had lifted considerably. She was glad she had met Corey. He was interesting. His extroversion did not bother her. She had never known a real live gay person before. And on top of that he was from Nova Scotia, almost a Newfoundlander like herself. She hardly thought it was possible, meeting him like that.

He proved to be quite a good neighbor. When Joan was having difficulty studying, he spent hours rearranging her seating and her lighting so she would be more comfortable. They hung around in bars – not the gay ones, he went there alone – and occasionally went to a concert or a movie together. Joan introduced him to her few trusted friends, even to her family. They all liked him. They considered him to be quite a character.

At Christmas time, Corey made good on his promise and invited Joan to Boston. They traveled together, those poorer members of the jet set. When they reached Boston, she met David, who was shy, charming and affable. Somewhat reserved, but with a tremendous sense of dignity. The three of them ate together in a classy restaurant, and the two men took Joan on a brief tour of the city's attractions, including its famous mall. When night came, she was bedded down on the floor in the living room of David's condominium, while the two lovers shared the bedroom.

In the morning, Corey said to her, "My dear, I'm afraid you're in danger of becoming a fag hag."

She didn't know what that meant, so he explained, "Oh, it's just a woman who hangs around with male homosexuals."

She laughed. "If I'm becoming one, it's you who are making me one." She didn't think it was such a serious defect.

As she got to know them, Joan discovered that all the gays in Corey's circle were responsible. They had high moral standards and cared deeply about gay lifestyles And at the same time, they all had heterosexual friends. They were a community with a culture of its own, open to the larger society.

Once, in a time of her own inner turmoil Joan considered the possibility of converting Corey. She was not quite convinced that male homosexuals had the proper perspective on women. If only they would see women more realistically, perhaps they wouldn't need to be gay. So, out of affection for Corey, as well as out of loneliness, she harrassed him about making love to her, feeling he might well succumb. It was then that he told her why he was gay.

He hated his father, who had abused him both physically and mentally as a child. His father, he said, "brought the whores home to lunch." This created chaos for his mother, whom he adored. When he got older, he ran away from home to a life of petty crime and theft. For this, he spent time in a juvenile detention center and was saved only by David, who helped him adjust to society and who put him through university. He was eternally grateful. He would never leave David. There was much more than just sex between them. Joan realized he loved the individual, not the gender. He loved David, and he would probably not love another individual in that way, not even any of those represented by the notches on his bathroom door. Not even a woman. After that, Joan left him alone, sexually speaking.

Gambo Whorehouse

Gambo, Newfoundland, is a picturesque little village stretched along the highway in a southerly direction from Bonavista Bay. In fact, Gambo is often considered to include the 3 communities of Gambo, Dark Cove and Middle Brook, in that order from the turn off point of the main junction, southerly.

Gambo has the distinction of being the birthplace of the Honorable Joseph Roberts Smallwood, who brought Newfoundland into Confederation and governed the province, along with his Liberal party, for decades afterwards.

To June, however, Gambo had a special, magical appeal. June grew up in Windsor, Notre Dame Bay, but her aunt Eva, her mother's younger sister, lived in Dark Cove, Gambo, commonly called Gambo. Summer camps for children were unknown in Newfoundland at that time, but it was common practice to farm out youngsters to one's kinfolk for summer vacation. Thus, June and her sister Frances were often farmed out to Aunt Eva for summer vacation.

Their first trip to Gambo took place by way of the narrow-gauged local train known as the Newfie Bullet because it went so slowly. The highway from Windsor to Gambo had not been completed then. Uncle Walt was at the railway station to greet the 2 girls in his station wagon. They recognized him from his pictures.

"You 2 girls going somewhere?"

"Yes. Your place."

"Where is that?"

"Aunt Eva's. You are Uncle Walt, aren't you?"

"And if I weren't?"

"Then we'd better wait for Uncle Walt to show up."

"Well, I am Uncle Walt, so climb aboard."

The girls clammored into the back seat while Uncle Walt brought their suitcases around to the trunk.

They drove along the rather twisting road lined mostly with bungalows and the occasional country grocery or hardware store. June noticed the ripening gardens and the grass, which grew tall and was not cut in lawns as in Windsor.

Uncle Walt stopped in front of a medium sized iron gate, attached to a white picket fence surrounding a very large garden filled with tall spruce and poplars, and containing not one, but 2 houses, one half-finished. There was also a shed at the far end.

"Welcome home," said Uncle Walt. "This is our new home." He pointed to the unfinished house. "We moved in last month. As you can see, it's bigger than the old one. But the upstairs, the bedrooms, aren't finished. The windows aren't insulated, but they'll do for the summer. You'll be sleeping up there, but don't worry, there are lots of good quilts and comforters."

June and Frances tip-toed the cement blocks to the back door of the house. Twilight was approaching. The back door entered into a porch and the porch door into a huge kitchen. At one end of the kitchen was a wood stove and hanging from the ceiling was a kerosene lamp. The stove was much the same as the one in the girls' house in Windsor, but the lamp was new to them. They were used to electric lighting at the flip of a switch.

Aunt Eva was busy flipping cod tongues on the stove. "I cooked your favorite," she said. "How are you doing, me duckies?"

"We're OK," said Frances. "Uncle Walt said we sleep in the unfinished beds upstairs."

"" Not unfinished beds, unfinished bedrooms. Don't worry, you'll be plenty warm."

The door opened, and in came the girls' cousins, Emily and Donald, who had been up at Lush's grocery store to buy potatoes. Donald slung the sack of them onto the chair nearest the table. "Here you go, mudder." He said.

The cousins had met before, but they had been much younger then. Frances and June both vied for the attention of Emily, but Donald, as a boy, was left out. He seemed, however, more than content to leave the girls alone.

There was one other cousin to arrive. Before he made it, the rest of the family sat down to their meal of cod tongues, potatoes, onions and snow peas. In the midst of this, in strode Evan in his oilskins and gumboots. He had been working on his boat, the Mickey, which was still leaking, in spite of his best efforts. By his side was his huge Labrador dog, Mick, all wet from swimming and matted with kelp and sewage.

"First thing you do is clean that dog," said Aunt Eva.

Evan grumbled and got out the tub.

Mick ran and hid behind the stove.

"Here, boy," called Evan. With great difficulty, he got Mick into the tub, and sat down to cold cod tongues.

Upstairs was huge. The master bedroom and 5 others. The girls huddled in one and were allowed a kerosene lantern to read by. Frances became quite unpopular when she accidently blew it out and Aunt Eva would not allow a second one.

Gambo was fascinating. Out back, behind the houses, was a shallow bog, leading to the beach, where June learned to swim that year. When the tide was in, you could swim right next to the shore. When the tide was out, you could walk way out to where the water was over your head. There was a large rock out there that the girls claimed as their home. They could all lie on this rock and get a suntan. On the walk out to this rock, or back from it, were kelp with mussels, holes from which to dig clams, snails, sand dollars, starfish, ossie eggs (sea urchins), even spanytickles in places. All these miracles of the sea intrigued the youngsters.

Behind the tracks, at the back of Gambo, were places for berry picking. Raspberries, blueberries, partridge berries and wild strawberries, appeared in season. On the bogs were little orange bakeapples.

The girls loved Gambo. They came back year after year, until finally Gambo faded into the stream of things, and life went elsewhere. Oh, they came back to Gambo, but now only rarely and for much more limited visits, usually not even overnight.

June ended up in the city of Montreal. Eventually, she had spent more time there than she had in Newfoundland.

She studied and held down various jobs. Before leaving Newfoundland, she studied in St. John's. She left high school in Grand Falls a virgin, and she stayed a virgin throughout her years in St. John's, though she had one serious boyfriend, a TV anchorman. She left him when he got too serious. In Montreal, she tired of her virginity and got rid of it with a Pakistani teacher. Since then, she had a variety of male friends and lovers, of various ethnicities. She grew older. For a very long period she had no one. She had a very good friendship with another Newfoundland woman who was married to a man who was half French and half Italian. The friendship ended in a fight, and for a long time she kept to herself. Her brother died, suspiciously, and suddenly her life was in turmoil. She had never found much consolation in the women's movement, but now it seemed utter madness. At the beginning of it, she had taken a job go-go dancing one summer. It was a light-hearted trip through clubs and bars. She did it in the country and learned oral French. There was no serious damage done to her, except irritation at too much impersonal touching at the end. She was interested in how the other girls lived.

Now, however, the movement took a new turn. It blamed her for her go-go dancing. It called it "showing off". Women should not do such things. In her day, no one had complained.

While the movement complained of her go-go dancing perhaps more than anything else, it also complained of other things. She had not gotten devirginated properly, which meant she and her devirginator had not stayed together into eternity. Also, he was a Pakistani, and therefore of the absolute wrong race and ethnicity for her. They had miscegenated, a crime against the movement.

Not only that, she had had altogether too many boyfriends. There was no hope for her. She was condemned to go back to the Gambo whorehouse and wiggle her bottom on a barstool.

Gambo whorehouse? "Is there such a thing?" she asked. "Gambo is such a small place. Anyway, I'm not going. There are lots of places around here with barstools, where I can wiggle my bottom if I want to."

She argued. For 2 consenting adults in private. She argued the value of her own erotic poetry, gleaned from her experience.

The message kept coming back, "Gambo whorehouse! Gambo whorehouse!"

She had had enough experience with sex that she knew she knew how to do it properly, in the fashion, it was claimed, of the whore. But to actually be a whore, with all her training and experience in other areas, would be a waste. Those movement girls couldn't be serious.

What was their sexual experience? She guessed, very little.

One day, as they screamed and yelled, "Gambo whorehouse" she answered back,

"Open your cute little leggies".

She had visions of them afterwards with their legs flying open in a scissors cut, not wide enough to let in any male organ. They had not gotten the point.

Anyway, it was just retaliation. Bend and stretch might have done better. But the Gambo whorehouse did recede into the background, as the little things maybe found someone else's mature sexuality to pick on.

I Love Her

I love her. It's the first time I've been so hopelessly in love with a woman. Well, not exactly hopelessly, that's an exaggeration. Hope has got nothing to do with it.

When I was younger, I did have certain attractions to women, but I dismissed them. I was more attracted to men. Also, I felt, strangely, there was some hypocrisy, if not lack of sexual freedom, in not getting involved with men._I started telling myself, and sometimes others, that though my sexual orientation was potentially bisexual, my sexual preference was heterosexual. I preferred a relationship with a man to one with a woman. I never sexually approached any of the women I was attracted to. I had fantasies about some of them.

That was a long time ago now. Partners have come and gone and I have remained – in practice if not in fantasy – heterosexual.

However, all that doesn't matter anymore now that I've met her. My bisexuality is no longer potential. I know I could have an affair with this woman, that I want to do that, and that the only barrier is that I don't know what her wishes are. I know now that one falls in love with the individual, not the gender, and that the individual can belong to the same or the opposite sex.

It wasn't that I suddenly met Sophia. I had known her for some time, certainly knew of her. She was a person in the public eye. I thought nothing of that at the beginning. To me she was then just a name. She was friendly on the few occasions on which we did meet, but there was nothing more to it than that.

The current phase of our involvement began when I started working for her on contract through another boss. That's when I fell in love. I don't remember how it all got started, but suddenly I was overcome. I relished her every comment, her voice on the phone. I ran to the computer every little while to see if she had sent me anything and I was disappointed if she hadn't. When I saw her "in real live person", a phrase she liked to use, I came home and daydreamed about her for hours. I could scarcely function for love of her. And this worried me.

I have a history of forced psychiatric incarceration and my main goal in life has become the prevention of any further hospitalizations. None of them had been necessary or productive in any way. I could not afford not to function. My history of psychiatry consisted largely of being picked up from my dwelling by police and ambulance and forced to undergo treatment involving medication and other practices too gruesome and oppressive to be dwelt upon. I was incarcerated 8 times. After the 8th time, I made a solemn vow to myself to never again let my behavior become so strange that my rights would be abused in this way. Because of all this, nothing, including my love for Sophia, came above this goal on non-incarceration. It had been 15 years since my last hospitalization, but I still thought another one could result from my behavior getting too far out of line. This could happen through my obsessive fantasies of Sophia, which I felt could disrupt my daily routine and set me off on the pathway to destruction. Yes, it could happen. In all likelihood it had started to happen. I worried. Was I already acting strange? Neither could I stop the fantasies, though I lived with fear. What I could do was control them, and I struggled to do just that. I loved Sophia through the fantasies, but also in spite of them. I devised a strategy. I convinced myself my preoccupation with Sophia was not based on her real personality. I would invite her to dinner. That way, if she accepted, we could talk and I could get to know her better. Seeing the real her would put our relationship on a better footing.

I sent her an e-mail message. I simply said, "I would like to get to know you better. I am inviting you to my place for dinner. If you accept, I know it would be enjoyable for me, and I hope it would be enjoyable for you."

I was afraid she would not accept, but after some time, when she had prioritized her e-mail, she actually phoned me and said, "Yes, it would be enjoyable."

I was ecstatic. I asked her, "What would you like to eat?"

"Oh, it doesn't matter. I eat just about anything."

I got out my cookbooks and settled on <u>The International Vegetarian</u>. I sent her a menu by e-mail and she approved it. I spent the whole day before her visit cooking. Not that we were vegetarians, but the food was healthy. Nothing but the best for my love. She called me from the building next door.

"I'm lost. Where do you live?"

"Oh, just around the corner." I steered her to my correct address.

"I don't drink alcohol," I had told her, "but you can bring what you like to drink."

5 minutes later, she rang my doorbell and I let her in.

"I brought you this." Bottled water. OK. Good enough.

We sat down to eat. The first item on the menu was soup, baked in baby pumpkins with milk and bread crumbs. I had to bake it for a long time for the pumpkin to cook, and the milk got coagulated, so that it was more like a soufflé than a soup. It was very filling. "I don't know that I've got room for much else," she said.

"Oh, please, there's lots to come."

And there was. Chick peas with apricots, broccoli with yogurt, rice pilaf, a garden salad. For dessert, there was a humungous fresh fruit salad, with yogurt and honey dressing. At this point, Sophia exclaimed, ", I couldn't possibly manage any of that."

"I'll give you some to take home."

I could only find a small container, until I got the idea to empty out a larger one. "I'll put that in there, and that in there…" I calculated. She took the small container anyway.

After we had finished eating, we talked. I rattled on:

"Both my parents had eighth grade education. My oldest brother didn't go to university. Even if he had wanted to, there was no money available at that time, either from the government or from the family. My next brother got a scholarship handed down from someone else who had two. My next brother won the district electoral scholarship. Highest marks in the whole electoral district. My sister has a PhD. In immunology and she's a pediatrician with a specialization in infectious diseases. Me, I'm the black sheep of the family."

"Why do you say that?"

"I'm the black sheep," I repeated. "I have an MA in English, but I haven't done much with it. I've worked here and there, but I refuse to work at anything I don't want to do. We had a big birthday party for my brother in the Eastern Townships last year, and we all had to give a speech. I got up on stage and said I was the black sheep of the family."

Conversation shifted to male friends, past and present. Yes, she had had some. She talked about 2 of these, John and Dennis. It wasn't clear to me if they were lovers or just friends. John was in the past but Dennis was still hanging around someplace in the present. "Dennis", she told me, "believes that to be successful in the music business, you have to write your own songs. You shouldn't do cover tunes."

"But," I said, "in very old folk music, songs were written and sung by the community."

Sophia told a story about John, which had something to do with being in a field of jalopena peppers. I couldn't quite figure it out.

"I bet you didn't know I once worked as a stewardess with Quebec Air. It sounds glamorous, but it was really hard work," Sophia continued.

The conversation got around to drugs. "I sometimes smoke marijuana," she said, somewhat shyly.

"I don't," I said.

"What? I was sure you did?"

"I can't inhale. All I do is cough and sputter and spit. I can't smoke anything."

"We're gonna bake it in your brownies," Sophia muttered.

"I don't believe in punishing the hell out of anyone who does do drugs. I had a friend once, a very bright person who could talk on almost any topic. She had an MA in political science. She got into crack cocaine and I have no idea where she is now. I often wonder what makes people like her get into drugs."

"Pain."

"Kicks. I'm all for Libby Davies and the free needle exchange, though." Sophia was from BC.

"I even sympathize with the poppy growers of Afghanistan."

"Oh, I wouldn't go that far."

"What other kind of economy have they got?"

36

"I'm the oldest in my family," she said. "When I was a teenager, I used to get marijuana from my 2 younger brothers. When my mother found out I was smoking it, she asked me to keep it a secret and not set a bad example for my brothers, who were my suppliers."

"We didn't have a problem with drugs in my family, but when my father found out once that I was living with a man, he told me I was destroying Western civilization. I lived with that man for 2 months. He told me sex wasn't important and I should look after the housework. That wasn't why I had moved in, so I moved out, "I said.

As Sophia was leaving, I told her my last story, "There's a little boy in this building, who's name is Tristan, which is also the name of my cat. He doesn't understand how Tristan can be a cat's name, when he's a boy and Tristan is a boy's name."

"How old is the kid?" she asked.

"5." I said, to her receding back.

The dinner strategy seemed to have worked. I had gotten to know Sophia better. I no longer felt threatened by fantasies. That is not to say that I stopped loving her. That love became rather chronic. Most of the day I went through my routine activities and I did not think of her much apart from the routine telephone calls and e-mail communications that went on between us. But the mornings and the evenings were filled with erotic and other preoccupations. The evenings weren't too bad as I could relax then and before I went to sleep I indulged my fantasies without fear. I dreamed of making love to her, or rather with her. I pondered the differences between heterosexual and homosexual sexuality. I had had some very satisfactory heterosexual sex, so when I fantasized about sex, I was used to fantasizing about penetration. Not that that was all there was to it. There was also exploring the male body and being explored. That part I could carry over to Sophia. A body is a body, of whichever gender. I never minded oral sex with men, though I was never able to fantasize about it a lot. I never got off on swallowing sperm. It never tasted good to me. I enjoyed the rhythm of penetration and coming together, when possible. I knew that the clitoris could be stimulated externally or internally and, if desired, by the penis, and that this often resulted in coming together, which I found not necessary, but certainly desirable. I knew how to apply a vaginal clamp in order to facilitate this. I knew all this, but as I thought about it, regurgitated my knowledge, I felt like a sex manual. I had no real man in sight.

With 2 women, it would be different. At a pure bodily level. There mightn't be any penetration. I couldn't fantasize anything sadistic along those lines. There was not even a question of butch and femme. It was a question of personalities, equality, real love. I could picture her body, but not every detail of it. It was her mind, her words, with which she seduced me. She had a way with words which was different from mine. Which I thought might reflect her usage of marijuana. She often meant several things at the same time, which to me was poetry, not ambiguity. As far as having sex with her was concerned, it would probably be a matter of who did what for whom. As it would be in other things. As it was in real life, in the real world.

These nocturnal fantasies of Sophia did not interrupt my daily functioning. I could live with them without fear of a destabilization.

Mornings were another story. It regularly takes me at least 2 hours before I am functioning normally then. 2 hours in which I am always tired, or depressed, or both. I get a little paranoid. I worry about what I might have done to arouse the anger of others, even Sophia. Sophia has never actually been angry with me, never rejected me. But in the mornings, I feel it is all a game, particularly on my part. She is probably not in love with me, not the way I am with her. I tell myself that true love is unconditional that I must love her, even if she has faults, in spite of them. I refuse to reject her.

I wonder how long the infatuation will go on. I know I won't be able to break it off unless it is broken off by external factors. Then and only then will I possibly be free to love someone else, male or female, should they appear on the horizon with all the particular baggage involved in a new relationship. The dinner worked. I have a better picture of Sophia now. I no longer fear that my fantasies will get out of line. I can cope, though she still preoccupies me. No other lover has yet appeared.

The Toilet Seat Position

They weren't exactly lovers though they were male and female and aware of that fact. They were a little more than friends.

Lucy would have liked it to be more than that. She had been alone a very long time and she had a weakness. She more than wanted to be in a relationship with a man. At times she was obsessed with it to the point of almost rendering herself non-functional.

Brad, on the other hand, had recently been released from the long-time clutches of a manipulative female, or so he judged her. The sex had been good, but he found no compensation in that at the moment. True, she had left him, but in reality both had escaped from stifling prisons.

"She was liberated, but I wasn't," he mumbled. "She believed in unconditional love," he said.

"That's something you give your pet."

"If Fluffy pees all over the place......" he began but didn't finish.

"Unconditional love. It's all right as a goal, but very difficult to sustain."

"Well, she was passive-aggressive anyway. Me, I'm assertive."

"I've never understood passive-aggressive."

"She won't talk to me."

"She could be defensive."

"Anyway, I'm not going back to her. We're divorced."

"Was that difficult?"

"No. We were never married."

"You called her your wife."

"Common-law".

"Oh."

Though he never admitted it, Lucy knew that the pain went deep. She kept her distance. This might not be the right man for her. Not yet."

"My religion," he said, "is kindness. My ex is an infidel."

They shared a few encounters, a few exquisite moments. She told him an old story of psychiatric incarceration. He was planning to come see her but he came down with a migraine, acute sinusitis and temporary hearing loss, in that order. When he was better, she took him out to dinner. He never got to hear her stories.

He also got more superficial, more banal. She had been intrigued by his uninhibited expression of his feelings, on everything, not just her. "Have your emotions, don't let them have you!" he liked to say. Now he showed his passion less often. He stuck to opinion. His facts were good enough, but he supplemented them more with cliché now, less with genuine understanding.

This Lucy found frustrating. She had liked his feelings. They were generally right on. Now they skirted around the issues of women and men and he told her,

"I give women what they need, not what they say they want."

She had had enough. Her loneliness and frustration came to the fore. Her sexual longing.

"How do you know what I need?" she cried. "And might it not sometimes be the same as what I want? Really, women are grownup people!"

This caught him off guard. His feelings came back, his genuine feelings. But they were darker than she had ever seen them before.

"Women, grownup!" he sneered. Why is it that you women make such a fuss about the toilet seat position? Obviously, you need it down."

"Usually," she countered, "I do not pee standing up. But at the times when I have accidentally peed my pants, I have done so. Which proves that I do not need the toilet seat down, though it is more comfortable that way.

Women and men are, by definition, adults, though some individual specimens may not behave as such. My father taught me that men and women are equal, and I won't let any younger man say differently."

After that, he wrote her a letter in which he told her,

"I am beginning to speak female. I do not understand womanese but I am learning to speak female."

She wasn't convinced, "You still do not understand womanese very well and neither do you speak female well despite your efforts."

Angel and Jessica

I love my community. I don't always understand it, but I love it. I volunteer in several organizations, which help me understand it better, but the more I do, the vaster the community seems, and my understanding palls before the vastness.

Each year, the Community Council sponsors a huge free turkey dinner on Christmas Day, for the community as a whole, but especially for the poor and the homeless. The organizers of the dinner approach certain citizens to cook and/or buy turkeys for the event. This year, I bought a $94, 13 kg. turkey and cooked it on Christmas morning. Otherwise, I had Christmas with family on Christmas Eve. My sister-in-law was leaving for India on Christmas Day. My turkey was my contribution to the community at large.

Paul was in charge of the community dinner. He came to my place to collect the turkey after it was roasted. He suggested I invite other people in my building to the Christmas dinner. "James is already coming with me," I said, "but I'll go around and see if anyone else wants to come."

Most people were either out or planning a celebration at home. When I came to Charlotte's door, she had a cold. "What about Abigail and Erica?" I asked, "Would they like to come?" Abigail and Erica were Charlotte's 2 young daughters, aged 7 and 6 respectively. They were busy playing.

Charlotte asked them, "Would you like to go out to a Christmas dinner with Grace and James?" They were very enthusiastic. "Yes! Yes," they cried. Abigail, the older girl asked "Where is it?", and little Erica guessed that maybe Santa Claus would be there.

The family is from Ghana. Charlotte is divorced and she lives alone with her children. She is a new arrival in Canada. I helped her with information for her citizenship exam.

I had Abigail and Erica for tutoring sessions in the building. They were a delight.

They came to my place for the Christmas dinner in snow pants and snow jackets. They were both intrigued about and terrified of my huge, fluffy, white Persian cat, Tristan.

"I don't like cats," said Abigail, grimacing, but she kept staring at Tristan, who was sleeping peacefully in the Lazy-Boy across the room from her. "Is it all right if I go see her?" she finally asked.

"Of course it is."

Gingerly, she approached. Erica followed. They stroked the cat's fur gently and were surprised that it didn't even wake up.

"What's her name?" Abigail asked.

"She's a he."

"What's HIS name then?"

"Tristan."

"He doesn't scratch?"

"Not people. He's got a scratching pad."

James knocked on my door and we went off to the Christmas dinner. We walked to the bus stop and took the bus to West Broadway, where the Christmas dinner was.

"Today" said Erica, "I'm not Erica, I'm Jessica." I didn't ask why. I figured it was some child's game she was playing.

"I'm Angel," said Abigail, not to be outdone.

The dinner was in the basement of St. Ignatius of Loyola Church. Endless tables were spread with checkered tablecloths while elves in Santa caps scampered through the holiday crowds of families, friends and loners, waiting on tables.

We found a table in the front near the stage, and sat down. Abigail and Erica removed their outer clothing, including caps, revealing tight little African braids. All along, Erica had refused to wear her mittens, which were attached with a string, despite the cold. It seemed she didn't know how to put them on properly, and she wouldn't let anyone else do it.

Abigail and Erica, reminding us that they were now Angel and Jessica, picked at their dinner, but showed great interest in what else was going on around them. There was a pile of wrapped gifts on the stage. "Are they for us?" asked Erica. Surely, they were for the children. Santa had already left by the time we got there, but a middle-aged woman helper brought along 2 big boxes.

"Here you are, chickie-poos,"

The girls tore off the wrapping and found games with moveable plastic parts allowing for construction of objects suitable to their ages. Birds, elephants. dinosaurs.

Angel wanted to help out with the serving. "Go ask the other servers" I told her. She did, but they politely told her she didn't have to. A little white girl about Angel's age came over to introduce herself. She had been serving earlier.

Many people were awed by the little African princesses, sitting with a white man and a white woman. One elf referred to James as the girls' father. He swiftly corrected her with the truth. He was a neighbor.

When it was time to go, James left with 2 take-home turkey dinners, and I with one. Angel and Jessica toted their huge boxes. Jessica's was indeed too big for her, and she asked me to carry it. Even I couldn't do that at the beginning, but after I relaxed a bit and felt less pressured, I asked her for it. "No," she said stubbornly, and proceeded on her way. When we were near home, I was finally able to wrest it from her and carry it safely to the door.

James left us at a corner for another bus to the drug store. Angel and I walked on together, with Jessica trailing. When we reached the steps of our building, Angel and I sat on a bench there to wait for Jessica.

"She's slow," said Abigail.

"She's tired," I answered.

When Erica caught up with us, we entered the building and went to bed in our separate apartments.

Wop

Peter was the big wop, the silent one, but he could say more in a glance or a nod or a flick of the thumb than most people could say in a paragraph.

He was stubborn, but he was not cold. He was a very emotional person, and when he could not stand his emotions any more, he let them out all over everybody. This did not in any way damage them or his perspective, which was as rational as any ancient Roman's, and he tried to be just.

Carol was sympathetic. He was dubious about her. He liked her only when she was in a position of superiority and could save him from the judgement of his inferiors. Carol learned how to play this game. Peter fascinated her and he could turn her on, but she knew she must never be the weak one, for he might just kick her in the teeth.

Still, he was sexually attracted to Carol. He longed to have her, if only because she was his superior. He longed to drop the mask of Roman stoicism and play the mere Italian playboy, her lover. But it was not in his character to do so. He was doomed to be tough, to be the law maker rather than the poet.

Carol tried to follow his every gesture. Only that way, she thought, would she ever really know him. And she wanted to know him inside out. He operated in a world of gestures, before speech. In that way, he went back to a primordial universe, which most cultures had discarded. Only in his gestures could he be understood.

That was why she didn't bother to talk to him, unless it was absolutely necessary

In a world without language, the Babel of tongues, there was peace. And peace with Peter was something she longed for, something she knew, as others did not, could be easily achieved.

Her culture had some gestures, but nothing like his. She would learn a few more. from him. She would become an Italian if she had to.

It got to the point where he read her intentions that way. He would say to her "Italians are the best, aren't they Carol? Say it! Say it! "And she would smile, but she would not say it, preferring to appear cosmopolitan. In her heart, however, she knew she believed it. They were the best simply because they were what they were, a fascinating, multifaceted nation.

When Carol left the hospital where they worked, Peter stoically walked her to the basement lounge, along with his side-kick, Steve. She never saw him again after that. It was rumored he switched from studying medicine and went into engineering, but nobody knew for sure. She could picture his logical mind measuring beams and girders to make sure none of our great infrastructure would fall. But she never knew for sure if that was what he was doing, transformed into a modern Atlas of crankshafts and gears.

Tohry

Tohry is not an intimate friend of mine, though I am getting to know
him better. I know him from the building. The building in which we co-
exist. My apartment is on the first floor and Tohry's is on the third, so we
are not neighbors, but I have been here a long time and I know everyone in
the building except for a few new-comers. I like to think of this building
as mine in a possessive sense and I have a protective attitude towards all its
inhabitants. My attitude is not accidental. I am President of the Tenants'
Association.

Tohry is a somewhat quiet, shy man. He is of medium height and build.
He looks younger than his 40 odd years. His hair is a shocking black. He
is handsome in a boyish way. He is ethnically Iranian and Tohry is his last
name. His first name is Ashgar, but everyone calls him Tohry.

One evening last winter, I was alone in my apartment, engaged in some
of the tedious paper work which accompanies my position, when there was a
soft, rather hesitant, knock on my door. I opened it, and there stood Tohry,
looking pale and distraught.

"I am sick," he said. "I have no money." It was getting near the end of
the month, and the welfare cheques were not in yet. "I need money," he
continued, "for a taxi to go to the hospital. I can't go by bus. I am too sick."

"Which hospital?" I asked.

"The Jewish General. That's where my records are."

I had very little money myself, but I managed to come up with the $25
needed for the trip, and I gave it to him. "Here," I said. "Let me know how
you make out. What's wrong with you anyway?"

"I have colitis," he said importantly.

What the hell was colitis? "Call me from the hospital," I told him, and he was off, content for the time being with his $25. I wondered how much I should be getting involved. Was I setting a dangerous precedent for the other tenants? But then, I told myself, not all of them have colitis.

A few days later, Tohry called. "I'm in the Jewish General," he said. "They kept me here. I want you to come up and I'll give you the key to my mail box. You take out my welfare cheque and bring it to me to sign. Then bring it to my bank, take out the rent money and pay my rent."

It sounded like a tall order. A lot of running around, but I decided anyway to make time to do it all. Anything for someone with colitis. Tohry didn't seem to have anyone else to do things for him. He was usually alone.

I got the key, took out the cheque and brought it to Tohry. He signed it. Then I went to the bank. "I'm sorry," said the teller, "We can't give you any money. You can deposit the cheque for Mr. Tohry if you like." That was all the bank would let me do, so I did it. I went back to Tohry.

"It's OK," he said. "You did the right thing. I can take the rent money out of the automated teller here in the hospital."

We found the automated teller, but it would only let patients take out $120 a day. Tohry's rent in subsidized housing was $205.

"Damn!", I exclaimed, "I can't come back tomorrow."

"It's OK. It's OK," Tohry soothed. "I will call Ali. Ali will come. Ali will pay the rent tomorrow."

Ali was another tenant in the building, an affable and sociable Arab and Muslim from Iraq. A born leader in community activities. I hadn't known Tohry knew Ali.

I let it go at that. Ali was responsible. Ali would come. The rental office was not far from the hospital. Ali had a car.

Ali didn't go the next day, but the day after he knocked on my door.

"I'm going to see Tohry," he declared. "Wanna come?"

I had the time. He had a lift. It would be nice to go visit Tohry without the bother of taking public transportation. "I'd love to go with you," I said.

"I don't have much time," he explained. "All we'll do is collect the money, then go pay the rent. I can't stay long. I have to take Hussein to soccer practice." Hussein was his 11 year old son.

"OK," I said. "That's fair enough."

We went to the hospital, where Tohry was more than happy to see us. He gave Ali the money and off we went to the rental office. Ali parked outside. He gave me the money. "You go inside," he said. "Pay the rent and come back out. It shouldn't take you long."

In the rental office building, I pushed the button to the third floor. I had been through this ritual many times before, often enough for tenants other than myself. Ali was right. It didn't take long. I was lucky. There was no line up. Tohry, however, was 2 months behind on his rent. "Tell him," said the rental agent, "that if he gets 3 months behind, he can be evicted."

"Yes, sir," I said.

It was bad that Tohry was behind, but it was good that he was in hospital, as he didn't have much to spend his money on. Well, it wasn't really good he was in hospital, but the fact that he could save money there was good.

About 3 weeks later, Tohry came home. He seemed refreshed, relaxed, healthy. He had gained a little weight, but he was not fat, merely robust. I went to visit him at his apartment. He was cleaning out his refrigerator and he insisted on giving me everything edible that he could not use. He cleaned up his place and made it very neat and tidy. I didn't worry about him much for a while. I was busy with other things.

The Tenants' Association had been planning a major Middle East event, featuring the Arab and Muslim tenants in the building. On the day that it eventually took place, it was in the process of becoming a smashing success, with families present in traditional dress, delicious kebabs, oriental pizzas and baklava, as well as sweet and perfumy Arabic coffee brewed in special urns.

In the middle of all this gaiety, there came the loud blaring of police and ambulance sirens outside the building. There was a certain glitch in the party atmosphere as everyone wondered whom they were coming for. Who was not at the party? Tohry, of course, and there he was, white as a ghost, being wheeled down the corridor on a stretcher and out the front door by the ambulance attendants, with the police in the foreground. It all happened so fast nobody spoke to him, but the other tenants noticed that the ambulance attendants wore masks.

It took a couple of days to establish Tohry's whereabouts, but then it was discovered he was in the Jewish General again. I went to see him. His face was puffed with cortisone. "I have colitis," he said, "but now I have Chron's disease as well." An intravenous feeder dangled from his arm. "They want to do surgery," he said, "but I am too weak. I cannot eat, but they cannot do the surgery until I eat on my own, without the intravenous. That way, I would build up my strength and they could operate, but I don't know if that will happen. I could be on the intravenous for 5, maybe 10, years. I could die."

"You're not going to die," I scolded. "Just do what the doctor tells you. When you're strong enough, they'll do the surgery."

Meanwhile, back in the building, there were complaints about Tohry, or at least, about his apartment. They claimed it smelled. They were upset that the ambulance workers wore masks. They feared infection.

I went to Tohry and he gave me the key to his apartment. I went in there. It was not in a terribly bad condition. I didn't smell anything much. There were a couple of soiled bedpans, some dried food lying about, a faint smell of urine from one mat. The apartment needed to be cleaned, however, and I had no time to do it. I phoned the City. "We don't provide that kind of service," I was told. "Call the CLSC."

I did and was told they also did not provide such a service. "There are some companies that do, "they said, "but you'll have to pay."

I fretted about that for a couple of days until I found out that Tohry's next door neighbor had taken the initiative and called someone else in the City, who had promised to have the cleaning done, but she hadn't. "Would she?," I wondered. "Would the City allow it?" If we had to pay, we decided, we would pass the cost on to Tohry. He had nothing to do with his money in the hospital. Except, of course, pay his back rent. I called the other woman in the City first, however, and next day she sent round a couple of workers who threw out the used bedpans, spoiled food, soiled sheets and used Kleenex (which I had not noticed), along with the urine stained rug. Tohry's apartment was now reasonably presentable. No one complained of smells coming from it after that.

Cheque time came round again. Rent time. I had not been able to see Tohry for a couple of weeks because I had a medical problem of my own. Bad arthritis in my knees, making it difficult for me to walk. They seemed to be getting a little better, so I took the bus and metro and walked the dozen or so blocks to the Jewish.

Tohry was there, all bloated from the cortisone and convinced he didn't have much longer to live. He was still on the intravenous. He cheered up a little after I spoke to him and seemed happy to see me. He had not thought I was coming back. "I have been seeing my ex-wife, Noreen," he said. I hadn't known he had ever been married.

"I gave her my bank card," he added. "She will take the money out of the automated teller each day. I have enough to pay my back rent with a little left over. I still need you to bring me my welfare cheque to sign, and to deposit it in the bank. Noreen lives on Barclay, around here and close to the rental office, but she doesn't have time to go to our building, or to my bank, which is close to you."

OK, at least part of the work was done. I called Noreen. She was a sweet woman with a full-time job, as well as a teenaged daughter and an elderly father to look after. She had divorced Tohry 18 years ago, and had not seen him since then until someone had told her he was sick. "It is difficult for me," she said. "He wants me to come every day, and I cannot do that. I told him I will come when I can, but I have other responsibilities. It is very difficult because I have not seen him in so long, and I feel that I don't know him anymore. I will pay his rent for him, and see him when I can, but he should not expect too much from me. It is hard, too, for our daughter. He wants to see her, but she does not know him. He left when she was a baby."

I said I would bring Tohry his cheque and deposit it in the bank for him. Tohry had become almost like a cause to me. I had gotten to know him better and had gained another friend. I did not in the least mind the little favors I did him. It was worth it just to see the smile on his face, his sincere appreciation. I would continue to visit him, provided my knees didn't give out.

Teddy Bear and Bunny Rabbit

During her career as a graduate student in the English department, Gloria did some part-time work as a research assistant in psychology, where she got to know quite a few of the staff. There were two young professors there, who were exceptionally friendly. Allan, the older of the two, was in his thirties, divorced, and dating an Irish graduate student named Kathleen. Allan was basically a sober person, perhaps sobered by his divorce, though he was outgoing enough and not without a sense of humor. Jill got to know Allan and Kathleen first. Then she met Allan's buddy Stewart, who was in his twenties. He too had a girlfriend, who was extremely serious about him, but he fell for Gloria and would not listen to her refusals of his advances.

At first, Gloria wasn't interested. Stewart was overweight and he had just recovered from a psychiatric crisis. He was on a lot of medication. His speech was slurred and his behavior was lethargic. But still, he had a kind of boyish charm and an adolescent sense of humor. After he had pestered her many times, Gloria finally broke down and agreed to go out with him. It was then that she fully realized how little they had in common.

He showed her his publications. They were all on behavioral psychology. He had published quite a lot for his age.

"You mean," said Gloria, "you spend all your time putting rats through mazes?"

"Yup."

"Don't you get tired of it? Don't you think there's more to psychology than that?"

"It's my career," he said, somewhat defensively, "what do you like to do?"

"I'm studying the origins of drama. I like to go out. To plays. I used to act once. I even like movies and concerts, all the arts."

"I used to like that kind of thing sometimes too. That was before my breakdown. Now all I concentrate on is work. You know what they say, 'Publish or perish'"

"But you don't have to publish all the time."

"When I was in the hospital I found out how close I could come to losing my job, to perishing. That's why I'm not taking any chances."

They were in the McGill Sandwich Shop, his favorite hang-out, next to the A & W, which he claimed had atmosphere because it was frequented by teenagers. He was sipping a cherry coke, his favorite drink. He never drank alcohol, and rarely coffee. She felt like telling him how much he was like a gigantic adolescent himself.

He took her hand. " Come to my place and have sex with me."

"Are you nuts?"

"No. You don't want to?"

"What about your girlfriend, Sandra?"

"She doesn't matter."

She looked at him. He was attractive in his little boy way, but she could not picture herself having sex with him. She had the feeling that he wouldn't know what to do. That he wouldn't be any good at it.

"OK" she said, "I'll come to your place, but I won't have sex with you. Will that do?"

"It's a deal."

So she went to his place, and she did end up having sex with him. As she had expected, it wasn't very good sex. You certainly couldn't call it making love. Stewart was totally unaware of Jill's body, of any even slight responses on its part to his. He had to work so hard to get a climax that he was completely exhausted when he finally came. This was partly due to his weight, and partly due to anxiety. Gloria didn't ask him to please her, knowing full well he couldn't. She gave him what she could. After all, he demanded so little.

In spite of everything, they became a couple. They mostly hung around the McGill Sandwich Shop, and occasionally ventured to the further away A & W. They rarely went anywhere else. Those were the only places Stewart wanted to go, so if Gloria went elsewhere she went alone or with others.

They had sex in his place, when they had it. It was not great. It was not earth scattering, thought Gloria, but still, in her woman's way she believed she might get him to improve.

"I've broken off with Sandra, "he told her one day.

"How did she take it?"

"Terrible. We were engaged to be married, you know."

"No, I didn't know that."

"Sandra really wanted to get married, "he said. "She's a very old-fashioned girl."

Gloria wondered if she should have let herself get involved with this inadequate man, when perhaps someone else would have appreciated him more. But Stewart was old enough to look after himself.

"Bunny rabbit," he said to her one day. "You're my bunny rabbit and I'm your teddy bear." That was what he called them from that day forth. It was true he could be affectionate, but Gloria didn't see herself as a rabbit, not even as a Playboy bunny. She thought she was less objectified than that. The relationship invoked was far from the one Gloria desired.

She moved in with him. It lasted two weeks. At the end of this time, he grew tired of their attempts at love-making and told her, "Sex is not important. I want you to clean up the place."

That was not what she had moved in for, so she moved out.

After that, he no longer had a hold on her. She hung out with him sometimes, in the McGill Sandwich Shop. They had sex sometimes. She saw other men.

One week-end, he uncharacteristically took her all the way to the Chateau Frontenac in Quebec City, but when the sex got too frustrating for them both, he threatened to throw her out. For some reason, she found this amusing. She laughed and he calmed down and let her stay.

They saw less and less of each other and eventually they drifted apart. Years later, Gloria learned that he had moved to Ontario and gotten married there. Not to Sandra. To someone else.

Gloria felt a twinge of pity for the woman who had finally snared him.

Morning at Café Grand
and Salon Mila

I was up early and looking for a place to have coffee before going to my appointment at Salon Mila. Pizza Pizza wasn't open. I hadn't really expected it to be. It serves mostly pizza and isn't really in the business, I guess, of breakfast or coffee. I walked along Sherbrooke Street, heading east, 'til I came to one of my favorite restaurants, Subway. Surely I could get a coffee there. I knew they were open for breakfast. It was 9 AM. The sign on the door said open at 8. But it was closed. Locked. No one there. I don't know why.

I continued walking east along Sherbrooke, hoping I'd find a coffee shop somewhere in the vicinity of Salon Mila. I arrived at Salon Mila and right next door on the east side was this new looking place called Café Grand. I tried the door. It was open. I went in and a man who looked as if he were in his thirties, tall, with brown curly hair and the beginnings of a beard, was standing behind a long counter down the length of the café.

"I'll have a coffee," I said.

"Filtered, vanilla hazelnut, or fair trade?" he asked.

My taste buds got the better of my social consciousness.

"Vanilla hazelnut." I replied.

"Small, medium or large?"

"Small."

"Cream or milk?"

"2 milk. Oh, and do you have artificial sweetener?"

"On the counter behind you."

I picked up the sweetener – 2 packs – and turned around. He had poured my coffee into a fancy curved transparent glass with a handle, and was adding the milk.

I had deposited my bag, jacket and scarf at an empty table when I had come in. Most of the tables in the café were empty.

"I'll bring it over to you," he said. "It's hot."

I went and sat at my table. He brought the coffee and I sipped at it. It was hot.

"Been here long?" I asked him. I didn't know the area well enough to answer that question myself.

"Three weeks," he answered.

"That's not long. Do you know any of the other businesses in the area?"

" Only the ones next door," he said.

"You know Salon Mila?" I was warming up to him.

"Of course. My wife and I and our kids have been getting our hair cut there for about 10 years." He spoke as of an old friend.

"She's good," I said. "She's very good."

"I'm getting together a business promotion with her and the flower shop." He seemed confident.

"Will you put it in the mailboxes?"

"We'll do it through Canada Post,"

I went on to tell him that Subway was closed for no apparent reason. He was surprised that Subway served breakfast foods.

I bought a caramel square with a chocolate coating.

"It's very sweet," he said.

"I shouldn't have it, then, but I will this once," I replied.

It was very sweet.

As I was leaving, he said to me, "Good luck with your hair." I laughed and went next door to Salon Mila

Toni, my hairdresser, was there. "You don't mind waiting, do you?" she called from the back. "I've got a couple of people I have to do ahead of you."

I did, mind, a bit. I had been right on time for my appointment. But I shouted back, "Oh, no. It doesn't matter. Go ahead. I'm not in a big hurry."

Before Toni started in on the customers, however, the guy I had spoken to in Café Grand appeared. "Three coffees with cream and sugar," he said.

So I had to wait as well while Toni and the 2 other customers drank their coffees, before Toni started in on their hair.

I didn't really mind. I had patience. Toni was good. She was worth waiting for. WhileI sat there, I reminisced about how I got to be in Salon Mila in the first place. It had started last year at Christmas time. I had had no appointment and was frantically looking for someone to take me. I tried my usual Iranian place, but they just brushed me off with "Sorry, we're full." I went up and down the length of Sherbrooke Street with no luck, until I spotted tiny Salon Mila, tucked away between a florist's shop and what was then a vacant restaurant. I went in. The place was exquisitely decorated for Christmas with a huge tree in the middle of its tiny floor, and mock gifts all around it. On the walls were pictures and posters of Italy. A youngish woman in a lab coat approached me.

"What can I do for you?" she asked.

"I hope you can take me. Everybody else is full. I really need to have my hair done for Christmas."

"I can take you," she said, " but you'll have to wait. There are a lot of people ahead of you."

"That's OK. I'm not in a hurry," I was relieved she could do it. "How much do you charge?" I asked.

It was a little more than I normally paid, but I had no choice. I was glad she could do it.

Toni, for that was her name, was of medium height, somewhat on the stocky side, and she wore her straight blonde hair in a ponytail perched pertly on top of her head. This made her look younger than her actual years. She spoke to some of her customers in a language I recognized as Italian from the flow of it, though I didn't understand a word. When at last it came my turn to be serviced, she spoke to me in perfect English, as at the beginning. In fact, she was quite chatty. "How is your family?" she wanted to know.

"Oh, I'm not married." I replied.

"You don't get lonely?" she inquired.

"Oh, no. They say girls always get married, but in my family the boys got married and the girls didn't. I think it's to a man's advantage to get married, but not to a woman's."

"I agree with you there," she said. "But some women, some men, too, regret it if they don't get married."

"I suppose. I don't regret it though."

"Your parents?"

" Oh, they're both dead. I've got 3 brothers and one sister. I don't think my sisters in law mind being married. One is German and one in Hungarian, so we have a mini United Nations in the family."

"I've got German and Hungarian among my customers," she smiled.

In the midst of all this talk, she did an excellent job, snipping off just the right amounts from the sides and back of my hair, and from my bangs.

This year, I made an appointment. I arrived to an almost empty salon. Again, Toni did an excellent job, and the conversation was equally excellent. We talked about my boss, who had also been a customer of Toni's a few times. We talked about hair.

"When I was a child," I said, "my mother insisted on doing my hair in ringlets, which she had to glue in, as it was so straight."

"With Dippety-Do?"

"That wasn't around at the time. It was something stronger, I think." I laughed at this vanity of my mother's, for my sake.

"You know," said Toni, "your hair is fine, but it looks a little flat. If you come in sometime after the holidays, I could put a rinse in it for you."

That was what my appointment today was all about. The rinse.

The 2 customers who were ahead of me were younger and older. Toni did the older woman first, putting in rags I didn't quite get the point of, but the woman did turn out with a lovely blonde curly mop. The younger woman had just a cut. Her hair was darker but equally curly. They talked a lot about school, particularly school buses and school uniforms. They wanted to hire a school bus for a social event. I told them Transco did that. The younger woman, Wendy, was on a committee to order school uniforms. She said, "I have 3 children in school, and I prefer them to be in uniform every day. That way, you don't have to worry about whether what they're wearing is OK." The older woman, Barbara, was not so outspoken.

As they were leaving, "Toni said to me, "They're a mother and daughter team They came all the way from Pointe Claire. I had to do them first."

Her tiny Salon was filling up. A technician, also in a white lab coat, arrived.

Toni did take me next. She made me sit at a chair near the counter and she squeezed some gooey stuff into my hair. Not before she had gotten me to choose a color for myself

"I don't think you should go for a blonde, blonde," she said. Instead, she showed me a beautiful ash blonde that we both instantly agreed was "perfect". Then she rubbed it into my hair.

Again, I had to wait while she prepared the other customers. After about half an hour, she washed my hair. She had also put some of the stuff on my eyebrows, and she washed them as well. Then she blow-dried everything. The result was exquisite.

I put on my boots and jacket and went over to pay her.

"How much do I owe you?" I asked.

"$25." She said.

" Shall I give you $30, for a tip?"

"No, just $25."

"Are you sure you don't want $5 more?"

"No," she said, "but I want you to come back."

She had told me the rinse would wash out in 3 or 4 weeks, and that if I kept coming back to have it reinforced, it would eventually be more permanent.

I left Salon Mila knowing I would go back, knowing that Toni had become my regular hairdresser.

I went down the street to the Greek restaurant there, and had souvlaki for lunch.

The Loss of a Spouse

Catherine got up early that morning and, due to her considerable neuroses about being confined, went out of the door early, on her way to her appointment with the podiatrist, Dr. Williams. She was in such a hurry to get away that she was actually over 2 hours early for the appointment as she got off the bus. She went to the Second Cup on the corner and ensconced herself on one of the thick padded benches against the window, with a steaming hot coffee. She read some more of her book, *River of the Brokenhearted*, by David Adams Richards. It had been recommended to her by her friend, Julie, but she had been having some difficulty getting into it. Richards' style was less straightforward than that of Isabel Allende, whose novel, *The Infinite Plan*, Catherine had just finished reading. She was having difficulty concentrating. This was not unusual for her in the mornings. It took her a long time to get started then, to get over depression and anxiety. Especially during the early mornings. There was no cure for it but to wait 'til the mood wore off.

She struggled with the damn book, thinking on the side of all the meetings she had recently attended. These had involved various community actions and had been characteristically productive. Now all she could think of was that they were over. She felt bitterly alone and saw no remedy for this state. It wasn't true that she had no friends. She was a very sociable person. But in the early morning funk that seemed unreal. It didn't matter. She longed for intimacy. She wanted a romantic partner. She was so desperate she wanted to go out on the street and grab someone, but she knew she couldn't do that. There was no way out. The singles clubs were cesspools of alienation and the other night clubs bastions of cheap one-night stands as well. Catherine had always believed one met people in one's day to day life, but she had been waiting for years.

15 minutes before her appointment, she left and went to Dr. Williams' clinic. Everything seemed pretty normal. The pleasant receptionist - there seemed to be a different one every time – waved her in and drew the usual pan of hot, soapy water for her feet.

"That's great!" Catherine exclaimed as she let the feet slowly sink in, "As usual."

The receptionist smiled. Catherine wasn't sure she needed these treatments, but she enjoyed them. She had first come to Dr. Williams for ingrown toenails, but had stayed because of diabetes.

Out of the corner of her eye, Catherine saw the notice board outside Dr. Williams' inner office. There was something different about it. On closer inspection, it was covered from top to bottom with sympathy cards. On one or two of them she saw the word "wife".

Dr. Williams entered the examining room, where Catherine was busy removing her feet from the now tepid water, with the aid of the receptionist.

"My wife died." He announced.

"So I see," said Catherine, "I'm sorry. How old was she?"

"Old enough," he replied, "She had cancer. It was diagnosed last November. She died March 30." Since Catherine's last appointment.

"Cancer is a horrible thing, "Catherine commented." I used to work with a husband and wife team, who died within 2 years of each other, both of cancer."

Dr. Williams was still. He did not seem comforted. In fact it seemed he may have been contemplating his own death, in the wake of his wife's.

He was sad. Normally, he joked with Catherine. He got a kick out of the fact that she was a Newfoundlander. Now, he said, "I'se the bye", as he often did for her, but he was scarcely joyful.

"I have a new T-shirt, which says 'Yes, B'y' on it, she said. "I was going to wear it, but I decided not to. It was a bit too cold."

He looked at the beige woolen top and brown woolen pants she was wearing "Why not?" he asked. "Of course you should have worn it. Don't you think you could have gotten a good hot man to keep you warm?"

"My demons made me do it," she countered. "My demons made me not wear it."

She didn't mind the reference to a hot man, but she knew he was thinking partly of himself. He was not only sad, he was lonely. Catherine had not heard him speak much of his wife, but she knew he had always loved her, and was in deep mourning.

She didn't know what to do with him. It would have been sacrilegious, somehow, to have cheered him up. All she could do was try to sympathize. She had not known his wife.

Normally, he was cheerful. Even in grief, he maintained a sense of humor, but it was painful for him. He had, it seemed, an understandably deep case of the blues. He was black and felt the pain of loss deep in the depths of his African soul.

"You know," she said to him, "You can say 'Yes, b'y' to anybody, but if it's a woman you can also say, 'Yes, maid'."

As she was leaving, he said to her, "I'm going down near your place in June."

"Vacation?" she asked hopefully.

"Yes, maid," he answered.

"Cape Breton?" She knew he often went there.

"Yes, maid," he said again, and he was very serious.

She beat it.

Out on the street, she could not forget him, how he had been that day. His sadness, his profound loneliness. She knew he wanted her, wanted something from her She remembered her own loneliness, earlier in the morning.

It was too early. Too early for anything. He had to heal.

Did she want him? What a disruption he would be in her life, but he did love her, she knew he did. He loved her as a Newfoundlander, at least, and you couldn't say that for everybody.

He probably had had a very conventional wife. He probably would need another one eventually. Catherine was a mess as a housekeeper and he was a doctor, needing a woman who would be glamorous in public, not the raggedy and perpetually busy community activist she was. The fact that he was black was of minor significance, she felt, in the light of conventions and status.

Was he too old for her? She was not all that young, but she was used to looking at younger men, men who ran in the same informal circles of social activism as she did. She could imagine herself, say sometime in July, out on a date with Dr. Williams, a date in which they could possibly decide they had absolutely nothing in common.

"It's too early for all this," she thought. "Far too early. He's going on a fishing trip, that's all. When he comes back, he'll be a changed man. He probably won't need me then and I can be free to dream of someone else."

Effects of a Friendship

They met a long time ago now, in a little Spanish restaurant on Park Avenue known as the El Gitano. It was frequented at the time mostly by graduate students from McGill. Judy was a graduate student. Ruth was not, though she was the wife of one. Judy will always claim that she associated with Ruth because she had never been taught not to associate with anyone with an Italian last name. The fact that Ruth, like Judy, also came from Newfoundland solidified the arrangement.

It was Ruth's married name that was Italian of course. Her maiden name didn't matter. Her husband's father was the true, ethnic, Italian, but his mother was French and Jean-Paul had been brought up a francophone. His English was good enough to get him into McGill as a PhD. student in anthropology, though he spoke it with a heavy Québeçois accent.

Jean-Paul did not hang around El Gitano's. "He has his own places, like Casa Pedro's", Ruth confided. "It's very private."

Ruth liked the crowd at El Gitano's. She loved to hang out there, eating steak sandwiches, conversing with the intellectuals, and sometimes even picking up men. Judy knew of a few guys who had had affairs with her, for she was petite and pretty, with long blond hair and beckoning blue eyes. Her mouth was a little broad, but not enough to mar her overall beauty. She could easily pick up men if she wanted to, and she did want to, because she was not entirely satisfied with her marriage to Jean-Paul.

Judy was drawn to Ruth as to a lantern. Ruth was sweet and receptive. A good listener. She listened ever so patiently as Judy recounted the outline of her thesis, and she added comments which were helpful and insightful. Judy had not gotten that kind of attention even from her thesis director.

Ruth had only a couple of years' courses from Memorial University and a couple of years' teaching experience at a high school in St. John's. These days, she was mostly at home, caring for her young son, Francois.

Most of Judy's friends accepted her friendship with Ruth. They moved in the same circles. Some, however, never saw the significance of their both being Newfoundlanders. One day, they met another graduate student in a drug store and she was taken aback,

"You two, together!"

"Roxanne," Judy responded, "The last time I saw you you were working for Black Rose Books!".

"Day-a-lets for children!" Ruth shouted across the counter.

In the summers, Jean-Paul worked as a civil servant in Ottawa, for the native peoples. In that summer of 1973, Ruth asked Judy if she would sublet their apartment from her. The cost would be minimal but "We want someone in there we can trust." Judy was happy to oblige. She lived in a tiny room in a rooming house, and the thought of having the spacious 5 and a half, if only for a few months, made her mouth water. There, she could really lay out her thesis materials properly. Then,

"Hey, wait a minute!" she cried, "My sister is coming back from Africa through France soon, with a couple of French friends who need a place to stay. Maybe we can share. They're professionals, so that way you wouldn't be losing any money."

"O.K., but you're in charge. I don't know them but I do know you, and I trust you. That's what's important to me. I don't care that much about the money."

Judy, Mireille and Antoine all moved into the sunny apartment in Park X, just north-east of the McGill student ghetto. Judy worked at the Laurentian Hotel that summer, as a chambermaid. There was a minor squabble with Mireille over a hair dryer, but, apart from that, she was comfortable with the two French citizens. Mireille was a psychiatrist, but Antoine was unemployed. At the end of the summer, he went back to France, and Mireille moved to a smaller apartment in St. Louis Square. Judy went to another rooming house, this time on Aylmer St..

When Christmas came around, both Judy and Ruth returned to Newfoundland to spend time with their respective families. But since Ruth was from St. John's and Judy was from the interior, they did not see each other in Newfoundland. Judy did tell her family, "I have a friend from Montreal who's visiting her family in St. John's right now, much as I'm doing here." But she mainly kept this special friend's identity a secret. She returned to Montreal and her rooming house.

Ruth tried to ameliorate Judy's perpetual rooming house conditions by giving her a beautiful tortoise shell kitten. Unfortunately, Judy's room was broken into, and the animal was stolen after Judy had had it for only two weeks.

The 2 women continued to meet in El Gitano's, and sometimes at Ruth's place, and to discuss the mysteries of Judy's thesis. Judy grew more and more grateful for Ruth's assistance. She would put her name in the acknowledgements. There were other kinds of favors she could do for Ruth. When income tax season arrived, Ruth knocked on her door one evening and said, with a worried look, "I've got to go to my father-in-law's place on Louis-Hebert this evening, and I'm scared. Will you come with me?"

"Sure." Judy didn't think it was too much to ask. What could be so scary about the east end of the city? Jill had never been there, but she was ready for adventure. Ruth was wearing the dark green woolen cape that Jean-Paul had bought for her and in which she always looked stunning. It was also handy for hiding things under.

At Ruth's insistence, they stopped off at her place and gathered up little François. "He wants to see his grandparents". They took the metro to Jean-Talon and then the bus to the corner of Jean-Talon and Louis-Hébert. In the metro, Ruth bought popcorn, eyed the metro police, then gave Judy money to buy things. Judy couldn't understand why it mattered who bought what, but she went along with the game. What seemed important was the monetary exchange, that someone was giving money to someone else. That there was a little bit of a market place going on. The bus ride was a bit simpler, though the bus driver seemed to recognize Ruth. Like her he appeared scared.

From the bus stop, it was a short walk to the elder Rossetti's house. When it was in sight, Francois let go of Ruth's hand, pointed his finger to form a gun, and yelled,

"Bang! Bang! Bang!"

Judy ran and caught the child in her arms. He was barely 3. "Jesus, François," she said, "Are you going to visit your grandfather or are you going to shoot up the neighborhood?" The child laughed, but he enjoyed being subdued.

Inside the house, they were met by Victor Rossetti and his wife, Francine. He was clearly an extrovert. She, more reserved.

"I went all the way to St. Laurent Blvd. to get this," he said, as he served them wine and cheese, Greek olives, tomatoes, hot spicy salami and French baguettes. After they had had their fill, he complained that "the water was coming down", and told of how he had had to fix the roof. He was highly qualified to do that. He was a construction industry foreman.

Ruth claimed "You see, he's always for men, not so much for women." It was clear, however, that she liked the older man. Judy wondered whether she liked him even more than she usually liked her husband. It was also clear that Victor Rossetti was very much attached to his daughter-in-law. Ruth's own father was dead, and perhaps her father-in-law replaced him somewhat in a paternal role.

As the evening wore on, Francine Rossetti brought out what seemed to be the main point of the outing – the income tax forms, T4 slips and Relevé-1's, Ruth was to take and process for the older couple. Ruth and Jean-Paul, with their university education. "It's messy," said Francine as she removed the carbon paper from the slips. But they gathered up the information, and soon they were gone, leaving behind little François, who wanted to sleep with his grandparents and was granted his wish. Ruth talked about getting out of her marriage. Judy went around with her to legal aid to see about getting a divorce. But the legal aid clinic was closed, or there was no lawyer available at the moment, or there was a long waiting line, or there was some other problem. Still, they did not give up. They kept going back.

"You've been loyal to me!" Ruth almost accused Judy1 one evening, across a restaurant table.

Yes, it was true, she had been. She loved her completely.

Judy had been aware of her own potential bisexuality for some time now. Ruth was not the first woman she had been sexually attracted to, but she was one of the first, and perhaps the one to whom she had felt closest. She could take her in her arms now, and help to stabilize her. She knew that she alone could give her that sense of security she had never had. She could make love to her, though she had never done that to a woman, and make her forget all those things that were negative in her life.

Judy knew she could do all that, but she didn't do any of it. In a cowardly fashion, she clung to her heterosexuality. Better to have sex with Jean-Paul even. He was an attractive man, and a successful one. Ruth thought it might be better between them if he quit his work. Judy knew he would never do that. She knew life wasn't like that.

One evening, Ruth went off alone to one of the sleezier Spanish night clubs at the end of Blvd. St. Laurent, and there she found Jimmy, a tall dark-skinned Latino from Colombia. She did not know whether or not she was in love with him, but she made an arrangement with him anyway. She moved in with him and brought along François. "You're lucky to find someone willing to look after the kid," Judy told her.

Judy went to the club with Ruth. Jimmy danced a mean chacha. He had much less education than Ruth, let alone Jean-Paul, but he was friendly and outgoing.

The affair lasted 6 months. Ruth was pregnant, too late for an abortion. She lost Jimmy. "It's sadistic!", she told Judy. Judy never knew exactly what she meant.

Ruth had nowhere to go. No job, no permanent source of income. No lover. Judy could not save her now, even if she had wanted to. She had no money. She could not care for anybody's child. Ruth went back to Jean-Paul, who took her in despite her pregnancy. He had always wanted her more than she had wanted him. She planned to give the child up for adoption, but at the age of 21, it was to meet with François.

Judy and Ruth maintained their own variety of a somewhat estranged relationship. Ruth was angry at her seeming defeat, her perhaps real entrapment. Judy was tutoring a Jewish student at Bialik High, who was being irrationally discriminated against. The girl did all her homework, was anxious to succeed, but nothing she did was accepted. She seemed banished without a reason. Her father tried to talk to the authorities there, but they ignored him. Judy got Ellen into Wager High, where attitudes were then much more democratic. With this accomplished, she stopped working on the case.

She rented a small apartment, a big improvement over her rooming house days. One day, Ruth burst into her place, furious. She spoke in a curious manner that appeared codified, if one lingered over the words. It was anything but straight, but it was also profoundly frightening to Judy.

"That's not the kind of people you should be helping!" That part was straight Then came, "From now on you're going to be seeing a lot more of people."

It seemed a threat, It was far too loud. It was far too angry. Who were these people Judy was going to see?

"Get out!" she screamed, and Ruth turned and fled, looking back only to say,

"I don't know what's going on!"

She was out of Judy's life. They passed each other after that on the street sometimes, but they did not speak. Years later, they met occasionally, but they were never again close. Jean-Paul crossed her path when she went to work for an environmental organization and met him professionally. When she said she would like to have coffee with him, he thought she wanted to talk about work. Ruth had a cancer scare, but the pap smear turned out normal after all, after Ruth confided in Judy about it.

Strangely, Judy seemed to come away from the relationship with a heightened sense of caring, not for Ruth specifically, but for all humanity. She felt Ruth had made her a better person. She did not go back to her. She remained scared. For her own peace of mind. But she later connected with a grown-up François on Facebook.

Draft Dodger

He came to the St. John's campus of Memorial University during the height of the Viet Nam war. He came from New York City to avoid the draft, confused and barely able to function. Marie, herself, was in the depths of confusion about a scandal which touched an apartment in which she had lived. Though she was open to the stranger, she still had a lot to resolve.

Yet it wasn't quite accidental that these two confused souls found themselves frequently together. They were attracted like iron filings to magnets, but they could scarcely think of sex, and she was still a virgin.

She wanted, above all, to prove her accessibility to this outsider. "I'm here!" she wanted to scream. "I could be yours, if you want me." She was wearing her virginity like a worn out article of clothing, perhaps a housedress, to be discarded. She wanted to break the stifling barriers of a Newfoundland only culture. To put herself firmly on the right side of the scandal that had rocked the apartment she had lived in, which had gotten an undeserved reputation for too many foreigners, drugs and sex. Geoffrey was just another foreigner, but that was why she wanted him. To prove to the world she was "one of them, as much as one of us."

Geoffrey appeared to like her. He followed her around, hung on her incoherent pronouncements accepted her intuitions. Then, one evening, they went to a student play together. The actress in the lead role was a sultry dark-haired beauty who unfortunately parroted her lines in a monotone and moved her arms flamboyantly when subtlety was called for. In other words, she could not act. She was a student. Marie did not expect more, but she commented to Geoffrey, "She's a lousy actress. I think I could do better myself."

"I didn't think she was bad at all. In fact I'd like to meet her." After the play was over, he maneuvered his way back stage and did precisely that. It wasn't long before he was dating her. Marie knew that she had lost him, but she didn't blame herself. He was so incredibly confused.

All over the campus, he gave speeches against the Viet Nam war. He invited others to join him and they came and they protested, especially the other foreigners and mainlanders and left wing students in general. St. John's could have been a mainland city, like Toronto or Halifax. It was getting more and more like that each day, what with the challenging of St. John's culture by those who came from away. Radicals, hippies, alienated youth.

Marie thought of the people who had hung around her old apartment. They were like that. Hippies, outsiders, though some of them were actually Newfoundlanders. She had left the apartment because she had wanted to study, and it was impossible to do that with all the comings and goings on. Her view was simple. She was not, though others had decided she was, a moralist. She didn't care what others did, but she had to have peace and quiet, to study. But Geoffrey was not that much like her. He was from the Big Apple after all. You couldn't get much further out than that.

Marie ran into Blanche, from the old apartment, on the street one day. Blanche had had a number of crises of her own. She had flunked out of pre-med and turned to Arts, where she wrote very good, but depressing poetry, mature beyond her years. "Hey, guess what?" she said to Marie, "Lover boy, what's his name, Geoffrey, got shipped back to the States last night. The Americans came and got him and he's back in New York City now in a psychiatric hospital."

"No! How could they do that. Of course he's only in psychiatry because he's a draft dodger. Couldn't the Canadians do anything about it? Couldn't we protect him so that he didn't have to go back there? He was even thinking of taking out Canadian citizenship. I know. He told me."

Geoffrey did not return and gradually Marie forgot him and all the unfairness she attributed to his treatment on Canadian soil. Maybe some of the others tried to do something for him, but Marie heard nothing.

Many, many years later, when Marie was in her forties and working on an environmental conference, known as The Green Energy Conference, in Montreal, she came across Geoffrey's name on a list of contacts from New

York City. Could it be the same person? This Geoffrey was in charge of a neighbourhood environmental organization on New York's Lower East Side. He was booked as coming to The Green Energy Conference. "Hey Georgia," Marie called out to her side-kick who was also from New York City, "ever heard of this guy, Geoffrey Salman?"

"No."

"I think I knew him years ago. In Newfoundland. I don't know if it's the same person. Same name though. And the guy I knew was from New York City."

"He's coming to the Conference?"

"Yes."

"I suggest you do nothing and find out when he comes. If he's the same person, I mean."

On the day of Geoffrey's arrival, Marie and Georgia met him at his hotel and they had lunch together. Yes, it was the same Geoffrey, seemingly a bit taller and definitely more filled out, and anything but confused. But he remembered all the old people at Memorial, the freaks and the foreigners, the radicals and the hippies. Some of them had returned to Toronto and he was in touch with them there. He remembered the brief role Marie had played in his life, and he was touched to meet her again. He was married now, settled.

Marie didn't bother to ask him about psychiatry, he was in such obviously good psychological health. Nor did she ask him if he had ever been to Viet Nam.

The Rolling Green
Hills of St. John's

The dream from which I awakened had me back there amongst those vivid, rolling and dissecting hills, green streaked with white of a surrealist's canvas. I was there with Marty, and we were dancing among the hills, joyously leaping, almost floating. At one point, he stripped off his clothes and we continued to dance, innocently, with no hint of sexuality. But there was no doubt about it, it was Marty and I, just the 2 of us, alone in our non-erotic but spiritual pleasure, and I was happy to be there, I guess.

What's wrong with this picture?

Well, first of all, let's take the hills. There are no such rolling hills of St. John's. There are some hills in St. John's. Some circle the harbor. Signal Hill, with its famous Cabot Tower, is the best known of those. But these hills are not rolling. Signal Hill is almost erect. It juts out of the landscape like a fortress. And it isn't green, even in summer. It is barren and brownish. The green rolling hills of St. John's are clearly the fantasy of a naïve and amateur artist. The white streaks in the hills only make them reminiscent of the kind of Crest toothpaste I am currently using, minty and flavorful.

How Marty got transported to St. John's, I'll never know. Chances are he has never been there. Perhaps he followed me there. It is highly likely we had, in the dream, decided to live there together in idyllic splendor, which seemed more like someone else's dream for us, rather than our own desire.

Pushed out of Montreal, we seemed to have found a heavenly paradise among the green rolling hills, but it was all fake. I hadn't seen Marty for years. The last I had heard of him he was barely off the streets, living with a couple of female roommates he scrapped with all the time. I had gone on to other lovers and fantasies. We didn't even hang together. I was not from St. John's, but from the interior. The lure of St. John's was doubly unreal, for him and for me.

The dance of the St. John's hills was nothing if not ludicrous. I have never seen Marty dance. He may well leap, but I do not when dancing. I am firmly fixed to the ground and in my body. I have no affinity for ballet, and I can barely even tolerate ballet jazz, with its monotonous pliez 2 3 4. I dance to music. I interpret music. I make up my own, unpremeditated form. And I have perfect rhythm. I have always had that. It was Pierre I danced with the most. We bounced off the walls as well as the floors of clubs, but we did not leap.

Why Marty took off his clothes is another mystery, for I did not take off mine and we did not have sex. He might have done it to exhibit or free himself. It was OK, but it played a minor role in the dancing.

Waking up to our little escapade on the green rolling hills of St. John's was pleasurable, was nostalgic, was an invitation for me to pack my bags and leave the city of Montreal for greener pastures, literally, or fantasy wise, for the fantasy was the literal color of the stripes of Crest toothpaste, white and green, and the taste of them as well, minty.

But slowly, the fantasy gets deconstructed and the reality of Signal Hill, St. John's, the fortress, is more pleasurable than a minty green toothpaste. The green rolling hills of St. John's, pleasant in fantasy, bow out to the real thing. All the spiritual leaping gives way to a dance more corporal and the possibility of real human contact, with a partner not from the past but within the potentiality of the future.

Christmas Humbug

It was my first Christmas humbug. Usually I get the Christmas spirit enough to drive everybody crazy.

I don't know when it started to happen, but now we are constantly being reminded that "for many people Christmas is not a happy time" or "for many people Christmas is a time of great anxiety" or words to that effect. Well, I guess that's always been the case. Doesn't mean you have to be sad. That's the true meaning of the Christmas spirit. You spread your joy around. And that's what I've always done, even though some people may have wanted to belt me one for it.

But this year there was no special joy. No reason for this. No sadness either. Just nothing. Just humbug. What are all those silly people getting so excited about? It's Christmas. Remind me between my work schedule and my exam schedule. The boss wants me to work overtime on Friday night. Gotta schedule my Christmas shopping sometime. Must send out those routine cards. I'll go to all the routine parties with the boyfriend I'd rather break off with. Can't do that now. Can't spoil Christmas. Bah! Humbug!

Of course I'll get together with the family on Christmas day. The conversation will be predictably clever. They'll give me money, which I need. Just hope they give me enough to cover the Christmas shopping. Humbug.

What will I get for everybody, anyway? No time to make things. They've closed down my favorite gift shops. Shall I just spend the whole day at the mall? Humbug.

It's the last payday before Christmas. I thought I was the only one poor enough to wait 'til now to shop. But it's wall to wall people out there. They keep streaming into the buses and they never seem to stream out! They push and shove and get into shouting matches. I tell this to Candice, who works with me, and she says,

"That's the Christmas spirit!" Humbug.

Christmas eve at Marie-Claire's place. Just she and I and the boyfriend I want to ditch. Usually she has a big party. But it's cozy this way. Marie-Claire makes us laugh. That's her Christmas spirit. Not so much humbug.

What's happening with the Christ child? I am definitely not a very religious person, but I was also brought up as one and usually I like to follow the Biblical tale at this time of year. At least a few carols. I know most of them by heart. Maybe that's just all so much humbug, too. Now I don't really believe that. That's just the way it is.

Finally, it's Christmas. I drag the boyfriend who's about to be ditched (but doesn't know it yet and anyway it might never happen – by God it had better) to my family's place for the usual indulgences. They think he's wonderful. Just right for me. They've practically adopted him. Humbug!

There are several guests. They aren't exactly yuppies. They're ouppies – older urban professionals. The conversation is predictably clever. My sister-in-law's cooking ranks with that of the finest restaurants in town. I overindulge and have to lie down for a while. We open our gifts. As usual, they give me money. Of course I accept it. I won't exactly say humbug to that.

Boxing day. I put pictures in my photograph album. Typical mindless Christmas time activity. Perhaps I am getting the Christmas spirit after all.

At night the boyfriend that I'll probably ditch comes to get me and we head for Steve's place. Steve is a lawyer. His niece is a well-known ballet dancer. I attended her wedding. She's there along with her husband and many other members of the family. They're mostly Ukrainians. Very good food, but I don't pass out this time. The husband of the dancer is a psychologist from New York. We get into a long discussion about psychology and psychiatry. Most stimulating event of the holidays so far. Does this qualify as the Christmas spirit? Nah, he's Jewish.

Couple of days at home alone mostly. A few friends drop by. I realize I don't have food or money to entertain them properly. They don't seem to mind. Somebody's got the Christmas spirit.

New Year's Eve. The boyfriend who will definitely make it through the holidays gets dragged along to Sylvia's place. I work with Sylvia. She's

German. There's just she and her husband and the boyfriend and I. Sylvia and her husband are vegetarians, but Sylvia ranks close to my sister-in-law as a cook. I overindulge and have to lie down.

Then I get up and we have German gluwine. We sit around toasting the New Year in with that.

Another few days to putter around and grumble about finances. I don't really celebrate New Year's Day very much. I call up Stuart (a friend, not the boyfriend who's about to be you know what) and he comes over. I don't have much to offer him but he stays for a long time and we talk and then have tinned beans and sandwiches made from liver and bacon spread. He eats this. He doesn't seem to mind.

Next day, I work five and one half hours for an old friend who's a teacher and we go to a restaurant and have Vietnamese food together. Good to see him, as I haven't in a while. He's the only person I know who always said humbug to Christmas. Now I know how he feels.

I take the money from the work and put it together with $20 borrowed from the boyfriend who does come in handy sometimes even though I'll probably ditch him anyway eventually. I buy food and drink for a party of my own which I am planning for Saturday afternoon. No kidding. I don't even think it will be humbug. I like all those people I intend to invite. Originally it was just going to be women, but Mike, the black guy upstairs, insisted he was going to crash it, so I invited a few more token males, including the boyfriend, of course. It turns out to be a very good party. Mike doesn't show up until the party is half over, but then he invites us all back to his place for West Indian food he's been cooking. It's nearly suppertime, so of course we all go. The party continues at Mike's place. Excellent food. West Indian music. The guy even has strobe lights.

After people leave, the boyfriend and I head off to another party for the rest of the evening. Mostly peaceniks. Another good party. More good food. We get home in the wee small hours of the morning.

Sunday. Last day of the holidays for me. Lying late in my bed, I muse perhaps it wasn't so much humbug after all. I get up and take down my Christmas tree. Good-bye humbug for at least another year.

"Any Mummers, Nice Mummers, 'Llowed In?"

That was what the song said, the song that was all the rage in Newfoundland that Christmas.

"Aunt Anne, you comin' mummerin' with us?' asked my niece Betty, who had married last year, and who was home from Calgary on a surprise visit with her husband.

"No, indeed I'm not," I answered firmly. "Anyway, Betty, nobody would know me around here anymore, sure. They'd be guessin' all night."

"'Spose you're right about that. But me and Randy still knows a few good places to go. And Wayne and Susan are coming along, too."

"It'll be great for Susan."

Susan was my grand-niece, aged nine. Wayne was her father. Her mother was Betty's older sister.

Mummering. Actually, though the song did, we had never called it that. Around our part of the island it was always janneying. But it was the same thing after all. Only why were those crazy Newfoundlanders getting back into it now? Trying to revive a lost tradition.

It must have died out when I was 11 or 12. I was never an adult janney, though I remember plenty of those coming to our door when I was barely old enough to remember anything at all. When I was supposed to be asleep in bed. It was different then. Costumes were cruder, nearly all home-made. A few bright colors, but the main thing was that every inch of the body was so well covered that unless you knew for sure that that was definitely Aunt Maude's scarf that that mummer was wearing, there was no way of tellin' who anyone was. Of course, it didn't have to be Aunt Maude wearin' the scarf, but most likely if it wasn't it was someone belong to her or someone she got around with. Betty was wearing a green jogging suit which in no way disguised her fully developed figure, and I felt sure that half the town would know her by that alone. (Although they might be polite and guess for a while anyway, just to not make her feel bad.)

"Bye, Aunt Anne," they chorused, as they piled out in long rubbers, thumping along with their long wooden sticks.

"Where are you going?" I asked.

"Well, we're only goin' to people who we knows well, eh? You knows how it is now, Aunt Anne."

In my day it wouldn't have mattered. Of course the town had been smaller then. Now, there were warnings out on the radio to only go to places you knew. There had been incidents of vandalism and violence. You couldn't mummer just anywhere anymore.

The words of the song showed that. They weren't any that we would have ever used. What you did, in my day, was speak from the bottom of your throat, with the breath drawn in so that your voice could not at all be recognized, and what you asked was "Any janneys in de night?"

The people at whose door you had knocked were quite free to say "yes" or "no", with no tricks of the Hallowe'en variety being involved for a "no". Sometimes one might ask "Any janneys 'llowed in?" but this was less frequent and the idea of permission was not the central one. As for the mummers being "nice" or not, who cared in those days!

Our mummers left at 7:00 PM, and they were back by 10:00 PM, Susan's holiday bedtime. Their cheeks were flushed with the cold and they laughed and shouted as their sticks pounded the front steps.

"How did it go?"

"Oh, my dear, we had some fun. The one they had the most trouble guessing was Randy. Some of them couldn't even remember what me husband's name was. They guessed me right away, though."

"I knew they would."

"How did you know?"

"Never mind."

"Some people recognized Wayne's guitar before they recognized him, but they were glad enough he brought it along anyway. At least most of them were. Old Uncle Sam Patey wasn't though. Only music he ever cared for is the fiddle or the accordion. Not interested in none of the modern stuff at all, he wasn't."

"And how did they treat you? Good, or not?"

"Oh yes, good. We had cake and cookies, and tea and rum and whiskey. Susan had 7-Up. There were candy and chocolates. You name it. Aunt Daisy even wanted to give us some of her stuffed moose heart to take home, but I said no. Figured she had enough of her own to feed with that.

But do you know who was really mad? Harv Jenkins. Don't know what got into him. Guess he must have heard those stories about mummers causing trouble. He was going to call the police on us as soon as we knocked on his door! So we had to let him know who we was right away. He was nice enough then though."

"Some people might be a little paranoid." I said.

"A little what?"

"Scared."

"Oh yeah. I heard there was a couple of fellows went mummering the other night and they beat up this old lady and took everything they could find. That was out around St. John's somewhere though. Not around here."

"This place will be as big as St. John's in a few years."

"Nah. Go 'way wit ya."

"That's what they say in the paper."

"That's what they said, you mean. The mill's layin' off people now. They know what's happening."

"Which is?"

"What do you think? No work around here. Everybody is headed for Calgary, or some other place, just like me and Randy did. Soon they won't have to worry about re-settlement anymore. Everyone will have left anyway."

"I hope not. There's too much that's good around here."

"Like mummering? Why you wouldn't even go mummering!"

"Yes, like mummering, if you like! But also like honesty and decency and friendliness. People relate better to each other here than they do on the mainland."

"Everybody says that about people down here, but I don't know about that. Me and Randy have been up in Calgary for two years now and we've got lots of friends there. Not all other Newfoundlanders, either. People are the same everywhere. They're all right once you get to know them. And if you ask me, people around here are gettin' worse. Why there's been more robberies just here in this town this year than ever before."

"I suppose you're right Betty. It's just that I don't want to look at it that way. I've got plenty of friends in Montreal, too, but somehow I always think of Newfoundland as something special. Something that never changes. Something peaceful and warm and relaxing to come home to. It's like a mother I guess. When I'm in Montreal and planning to come back here for a visit, I just think about that spare bedroom in your mother's house and I feel all warm and secure and taken care of and happy."

"Shame on you, Aunt Anne. At your age, wanting to be looked after! But I guess it's like that for all of us sometimes. I don't feel like that about home though. I come home to help mom out, or partly for that reason."

"Yes, and I'm ashamed of myself for going on like that. Let me help you out of your mummering costume."

"Sure, it's only me old joggin' suit. Do you think we should throw out these sticks, or keep them for souvenirs?"

"Oh, keep them. Who knows, you might be back again next year."

"I doubt it, but like you say, who knows."

My Underworld
Displacement Flick

I must have fallen asleep, though it didn't feel like it. All I knew was that I was transported from my mattress in my bedroom in my apartment on Benny Avenue to a room somewhere downtown. Upon reflection, it was the room on Alymer Street that I had moved to when I had moved out from the apartment I had shared with Vince and Florence Caprani, many years ago. Vince Caprani was in the room with me. We were preparing to go on a journey of some kind. There had been some kind of a dispute and the Jews had opted out. I didn't have a clear picture of who these Jews were, but it seemed they were NDG based.

The next thing I knew, I was in another apartment. It wasn't clear to me just what apartment it was, but reflection proved that it was the apartment which Florence Caprani had moved into after breaking up with her Colombian boyfriend, Julio. I was standing in my blue and white checkered nightdress, long ago discarded. My hands were straight down by my sides. They were red and filled with excruciating pain. I don't know where the pain was coming from. I kept repeating, "How long am I going to have to stand around here, with hands pained down, pained down?"

I was not alone in the apartment. At some distance from me, slouched in an arm chair, was an older, balding, man. He barely made a move and appeared to be watching something out of the window. I realized later that he was Vincent Caprani's father, whom I had met once.

After an agonizing period, I was released from my pain into a third environment, outside. It may have been winter, I'm not sure, but it was definitely night-time. I was wearing a wine-colored dress, which also has, in real life, been discarded by me some time ago. It was made of a crinkly woolen material. It had slits up the sides and a rope-like beige belt which made it seem somewhat like a Roman toga. It had what was not exactly a mini-skirt as it reached just above my knees.

I was wandering the city anywhere from Cote des Neiges to old Montreal, which was where I ended up. The streets were full of traffic, which included horses and buggies as well as modern cars and buses. Though I clearly came to what was old Montreal, the architecture there was very much like that of Nun's Island, where my brother lives. I stopped in front of a particular high-rise where I was attracted by what seemed to be a party going on. I went in. On the first floor, there were a lot of military men, standing around drinking. I asked one of them how I could get to Nun's Island, but he did not answer me. A loud noise nearly split my ear-drums. It reminded me of my sister-n-law, who teaches the deaf.

The main party seemed to be going on in the basement. I went down some stairs and found the place crowded with men and women, mostly young, sitting and standing around and making polite, cheerful conversation. I joined in and was thoroughly enjoying myself when I finally decided to go home. But I could not find the stairs back up. Every time I went towards what looked like it could be an exit, it wasn't, or if it was, tough young men would come at me with menacing gestures until I was forced to go back and join in the conversation, which was now beginning to be frivolous to me. Slowly, it dawned on me that I was in a brothel. Oh well, I was cool, I could take that. Maybe I was a customer. But would I ever get out? I looked around for my friend, Esther Cohen, who had supposedly died recently, but whom I suspected had been forced into prostitution. Clearly, Esther was not there, but the search for her gave some purpose to my own confinement.

The basement had several smaller rooms off the main one. One was suspiciously like the kitchen in my friend Adele's house. I was very thirsty but, though others were drinking, I was refused anything to drink. Then I began to get hungry, but there was no food in the place.

As time went on, people began to leave the party, particularly the women did, until finally I was the only woman left on the premises. It was now made clear that this brothel was an all male one. I was angry that I was the only woman left to stand up, as I had to, for the opposite sex.

In contrast to the previous frivolity, the brothel was now filled with an extreme amount of pressure, which emanated from a huge wheel above the ceiling, which spun down and down on all of us there. Still, I could not leave, all attempts to do so being met with menacing gestures. I had to keep up the frivolity with whoever was in sight, while couples paired off into the rooms on the side. The pressure was not only on the outside, but on the inside of our bodies as well. It got so I could no longer walk without stumbling into boxes or walls that appeared from nowhere. If only I could relax I could avoid them, but I was filled with tension.

I entered one of the rooms. I was alone there. There was a large mattress on the floor. I was exhausted. I longed to crash right onto the mattress, but I could not. Due to the tension in my body, I had to bend over three times before I could finally place myself on the mattress. Then I blacked out.

When I woke up I was on my own mattress in my bedroom in my apartment on Benny Avenue.

I am not a schizophrenic. I do not hear voices. What I do instead is think that I am thinking other people's thoughts. In this way, I get people on my wires and what they say then seems as real to me as if these people were with me in person. I conjured up Vincent Caprani in this way. "What you have experienced," he said, "is an underworld displacement flick. Displacement since, unlike in other dreams and drug-related fantasies, the distortion is with respect to place more than time. It's underworld because it has to do with the prostitution rackets, rather than the political underground, which is more interesting. It's always a waste when such underworld techniques are perpetrated on intellectuals like you, who could be working with the underground."

This dream, or fantasy, was experienced by me when I was taking no medical or recreational drugs, no mind-altering substances whatsoever.

Slack Jokes

When it comes to humor, Newfoundlanders are a race apart. It gets to be scary sometimes. Bourgeois society is not prone to humor, except in an escapist, alienated way. It doesn't understand humor as attached to real life, and this is the humor not only of Newfoundlanders, but of any traditional culture.

Mass culture has spawned the ethnic joke and Newfoundlanders, though technically not ethnic, are often the butt of it. Ethnic jokes are funny only to an unintelligent and uninformed mentality. They equate the stereotype with the truth and cause a great deal of cultural damage.

The traditional humor of Newfoundlanders, and "ethnic" jokes about them, are 2 separate phenomena, poles apart. This could not have been made clearer to me than on a visit of mine back to the province.

I was sitting in the cafeteria at Memorial University in St. John's with my younger cousin, Danny, and his girlfriend, Yvonne, when suddenly Danny began to tell Newfie jokes. I was amazed. I had never heard such jokes told in Newfoundland before and I was doubly surprised that a Newfoundlander was telling them. A young, perhaps naïve, Newfoundlander, but a product of the culture none-the-less. This young person was a third year political science major, but it seemed the politics of daily reality hadn't sunk in.

"You shouldn't do that! Newfoundlanders aren't stupid!" I said. I was astounded that he had dared to so breach the Newfoundland-mainland divide.

Yvonne had said nothing about Danny's attempts at humor, but now she spoke up, "Well, they're pretty slack jokes, anyway. Easy to know they're made up by mainlanders. Only mainlanders could make up slack jokes like that."

These days, Newfoundland humor is experiencing a heyday. Humor has always been there in the folksongs and ballads, in the expressions and dialect of everyday life in Newfoundland. But with the advent of television, a whole new genre of Newfoundland humor has come into existence. This genre developed rather slowly. When TV first arrived on the island, the phenomenon of Newfoundlanders actually performing in it was unknown. We were fed the standard sitcom and stand up routines emanating from the mainland. No one thought that our humor could be marketed. No one thought it could be developed into a saleable product.

Then a show called <u>This Hour Has Twenty Two Minutes</u> hit the airwaves, with the wackiest, zaniest comedy to come out of the East of Canada. The comics were all Newfoundlanders and their comedy was blatantly homegrown. The original 4, Mary Walsh, Cathy Jones, Rick Mercer and Greg Thomey proved that humor on television need not be canned or imported. Mary Walsh's comic characters, such as Dakey Duff and Marg Delahunty became classics, earning Walsh the title, according to some, of "best comedienne in Canada". In 2012 Walsh won a Governor General's Award for her work. Rick Mercer developed his specialties, rants and conversations with Americans included, which also became classics. Rick went on to further specialize his comic skills in his own show, <u>The Rick Mercer Report.</u> Cathy Jones became the member of the original cast who stayed with 22 Minutes the longest, dealing out the same quality of comedy she had done since her original shows and frequent partnership with Mary Walsh. Greg Thomey likewise kept up his act. The 22 Minutes cast has suffered several turnovers since the time of the originals, but its standards of humor have not changed. It is as funny a show now as it ever was, and it has earned its longevity.

One of the later replacements of the 4 originals on 22 Minutes deserves special mention. Shaun Majumder has proven himself to be of exceptional caliber. His comic career has travelled across Canada and even into Los Angeles. Like Walsh, he is adept at comic character creation, the character of Raj Binder being perhaps his best and funniest. Majumder plays the race card to the hilt. Son of a Caucasian mother and an Indian father, he shows that Newfoundland is no stranger to multiculturalism. He removes from the map the isolation of Newfoundland's past.

The rich face of all these professional comics is shown not only in Newfoundland, but across Canada and elsewhere. It puts Newfoundland on the map in a new way. The only danger is that this professional experience may be seen as just that, and not as a product of Newfoundland culture as a whole. Then, we have to go back to Yvonne's "slack jokes", and the kind of humor any Newfoundlanders can make up all by themselves.

I Want to Get Away

I want to get away. From everything. A complete change. I don't know where. I don't want to go to Newfoundland. All they saw in me there last time I went was someone who should lose weight. Apart from that a complete failure. I couldn't begin to explain my activities.

I thought about Rawdon. I like Masha Nedwetsky, Tanya's mother. She would probably make me comfortable there, though she is 82 years old. She desperately longs for Tanya to come live with her there and get rehabilitated. Tanya wants to live with Abraham, whom she calls her husband, common-law of course. The problem with Abraham is that he is both a street rat and a pack rat. I have seen the enormous pile of garbage he has brought home when living with Tanya before. Bicycle parts, motors, etc. He has largely been responsible for getting himself and Tanya evicted twice, though Tanya is no neat freak herself, designing ineffective roach motels out of cigarette boxes.

Perhaps Masha and I could together scheme to rehabilitate Tanya, though that would be a monumental task. And it wouldn't mean getting away from everything.

Masha alone I could take. I'd be able to relax. But with Tanya around, there wouldn't be any relaxation.

I've thought vaguely about Oka. It's beautiful there and I know no one, so the relaxation should be just about complete. Of course, I'd have to pay for my rest. One advantage of Rawdon is that I'd only have to pay for the bus fare up there, and maybe some groceries. I might even get a lift with Tanya's sister, Vaya. But if I would have to participate in a project to rehabilitate Tanya again - it wouldn't be the first time – that would be work.

Oka would be fine, provided I can afford it. I don't really know it too well, actually, not like Rawdon. Oh well, forget Rawdon, forget Oka. Perhaps I can dream.

If Gabi were still alive and the Auberge Alburg still standing, I could go to Vermont with her. It would only be a partial getaway, as there would be considerable talk and concerns about refugees, but Vermont is beautiful and tranquil. But alas, Gabi has passed on and the Auberge no longer exists. It was her American home. She was the owner.

I would really like to go to the Caribbean somewhere, maybe Jamaica, Trinidad or even Haiti, where some of the people in my building are from. I've never been to any of these places, but I have become familiar, through the building, with some of the culture from there. I know a little more than what is portrayed in the colorful vacation ads. But just because I do, perhaps that wouldn't be a complete getaway either. Besides, I couldn't possibly afford it, unless someone smuggled me, all expenses paid, all the way.

Where could I go? There is nowhere really. If I went up North, way up north to Nunavit, that would be away from it all as I've both never been there and know nobody there. It would be interesting. It might be cold. It would be different. Perhaps I could relax. But I couldn't really afford to go there either.

If I went to some small place just outside the City limits, it might be enough of a change, but I'd still have to pay the hotel bill.

I know, I could make a picnic and go to Beaver Lake. The swans should be back there soon and they're beautiful. It wouldn't necessarily be getting away from it all. I'd still have to come home to sleep. But it might be enough of a change to tide me over until I can plan something better. After all, the aim of getting away from it all is not to do so for its own sake, but to come back refreshed, to "changer les idées" as they say in French. It is to return better able to face all that you felt it was so necessary to leave behind.

Hors D'Oeuvre Buses

Waiting in the shelter for the 162 bus one day, I encountered another woman. She was plumply middle-aged and she seemed in a bit of a hurry. I always talk to people in bus shelters and at bus stops.

" I wish that stupid bus would come," she said.

We were out of luck. Buses came hurtling by. All with bright yellow "hors de service" signs on them.

"Oh, no! Not another hors d'oeuvre bus! " the woman exclaimed as the 3rd bus sped past,

The Montreal Public Transit authority, or STM, isn't totally unreliable. It has even won an international prize for its efforts in improving quality of life. It has increased ridership and plans to continue doing this, but roads and construction still make it difficult for vehicles, and hors d'oeuvre buses are far too frequent,

One wintry evening a couple of years ago, there was a tremendous lineup for the 162 bus at the shelter across from the Villa Maria metro station. It was cold enough to freeze your fingers off, even inside thick woolen mittens. When the bus finally arrived, the driver was met with lively condemnations.

"En maudit tabernacle! Where were you? You should have been here half an hour ago!"

"I had to go to the bathroom."

"The bathroom! It's 20 below."

" Hey, let me off here!"

"Can't. It's too slippery."

The grumbling, the chaos, kept up, all the way home, I felt sorry for the driver, and sorrier for everyone else.

In summer, you get the construction traps and detours, In winter, it's the snow and the cold, And through it all, there's plenty of those God forsaken hors d'oeuvre buses, offering no comfort as they speed down the street leaving you stranded.

I tutor 2 girls, Amy aged 7 and Jessica aged 6. On Christmas day, I took them to a Christmas dinner, and occasionally I take them on other outings as well. Sometimes we take the bus, when the hors d'oeuvre buses aren't the only ones running.

"What's a hors d'oeuvre bus?" asks Amy.

"It's not what you think it is."

"An hors d'oeuvre is something to eat, isn't it?"

"You bet."

"A small thing."

"Uh-uh."

"Mommy makes hors d'oeuvres for parties. But what's a hors d'oeuvre bus?"

"It's not a small thing at all. But it is empty. There's nobody in it except the driver. You don't get much out of an hors d'oeuvre and you don't get anything out of a Hors d'oeuvre bus, Actually, it is an hors de service bus – a bus that isn't running.

"I know that."

"Well, why did you ask?"

Jessica added to the conversation, "Mommy makes hors d'oeuvres with crackers and paste."

"Paté," said the all-knowing Amy. "Liver paté."

|" It's not liver. I hate liver."

"It is, too, liver. Duck."

"Ducks don't have livers."

"Shows how much you know."

"Only animals have livers."

"Ducks are animals."

"No they're not, they're birds."

"Birds are animals, dodo. Hey, that gives me an idea. We could make some really small cookies in the shape of buses, and serve them as hors d'oeuvre buses.

"But for hors d'oeuvres we should have crackers. Perhaps it would work, though."

"Hors d'oeuvre buses," I said. "They're all over the place. I wonder why that woman called them that?"

The buses were empty and inaccessible, 2 things which the STM tried hard to avoid. They were both of these things because of weather and the urban environment. The potential passengers were the losers.

Hors d'oeuvre buses and hors d'oeuvre trains. All part of urban transit. All going nowhere, but back for repairs. All inaccessible, negligible in current capacity.

Hors d'oeuvre buses are a common sight. Hors d'oeuvre trains pass by a little less frequently, but I remember one summer when they came in abundance up around the Papineau metro station. They jumped the tracks 5 or 6 times to land up on the opposite side in a kind of morbid dance while I stood awestruck and impatient, as I had very real things to do with more accessible trains,

"We could make some hors d'oeuvre trains as well," said Amy. "We could make some big cookies. Buses and trains. They wouldn't have to be hors d'oeuvre ones at all."

"It's just a name some woman gave the buses. Probably because it's known in English. 'Hors de' means outside of. Hors d'oeuvre is a special expression for party snacks. There's no such thing as a hors d'oeuvre bus, except in our imagination."

"Perhaps a hors d'oeuvre bus goes to a hors d'oeuvre party. But why doesn't it pick us up so we can go, too?"

"It must be a private party,"

" Hors d'oeuvre buses aren't very friendly."

"No. It's not nice to have to wait and wait and nearly freeze to death in winter.\'

"I don't like either hors d'oeuvre buses or hors d'oeuvre trains. I don't think we should have them."

"They're really only going to the garage to get fixed."

" That might be OK for them, but what about us?"

"We just have to wait for the real buses. The main meal."

An Equal Love

It seemed to Terri that she had known Martin forever. She admitted to herself that she did not know him well, but there was something in the way he looked at her, talked to her, listened to her, which made them instant soul-mates. Few men, few people, had the ability to do that, to give her, no matter what the superficiality or intensity of an encounter, what amounted to unconditional love. She felt Martin liked her not because of what she could bring to his career, not as a status or sex symbol, but simply for herself. It was not easy to find people who liked you that way.

Because he liked her so innocently, Terri was attracted to Martin, sexually as in every other way. She fantasized about making love to him, stimulating herself until she reached orgasm. She had often used masturbation this way, with other fantasies of other lovers. She was discrete about it. Nobody knew her secret, or so she thought.

Martin was an influential person. Terri admired him for that. They belonged to the same political party and Martin had actually encouraged Terri to become a delegate to the party's convention. Terri appreciated the backing. She picked up the habit of attending party meetings and often stayed until the bitter end of them. One evening in January, as she was dreading the long bus trip home in the snowy dark, Martin stopped her and asked.

"Can I give you a lift?"

Could he! He was never more welcome, though he was usually welcome. "That would be great!" she replied. "You don't know how I was dreading getting home in this!"

He lived not far from her, but she was scarcely expecting his generosity. He seemed on edge, stiff, formal. He made her anxious and she responded to his conversation with nervous laughter. In the car he was solicitous.

"Are you sure you're not too hot?"

She shook her head.

"If you get too hot just let me know. I can regulate the temperature."

" I'm sure I'm not hot."

They talked about issues that had come up at the meeting. He let her off at her corner, with an admonition to "Vote!", as there was an election coming up soon,

She had felt the tension as much as he had, but she had been careful not to let it show. Now, she ran though the snow to her building, to her apartment, where she unlocked the door and slammed it behind her. She stood with her back to it for over a minute. He had given her a lift home! He had conquered her. She was his. As she prepared for bed she kept muttering to herself "I'm your slut! I'm your shiksa!"

Martin was not only Jewish, but married. Terri knew his wife and liked her. Ordinarily she might have refrained from her passion for Martin so as not to hurt the deserving Sharon. But her passion was not ordinary. She would have an affair with Martin if he wanted it. No other man would do.

The next time she saw Martin it was unexpected. She was in a good mood because she had just come from a highly successful meeting of the tenants' association in her building. Everything had gone smoothly, there had been lots of enthusiasm about various projects and she felt proud to be involved. It was a little late, but she had been invited to a send-off party for Ken Cooper, a friend who was leaving to become a community organizer in Pakistan.

Terri walked the length of Monkland Avenue to the Olde Orchard pub, where the party was being held. Some people were already leaving, but there at the table sat Martin. "I didn't know you knew Ken," she said.

"Worked with him for years."

"That's an exaggeration," Ken commented, suddenly appearing from the bar area. "But yes, we're old friends, or at least acquaintances."

Terri sat down at a vacant seat at the end of the table, slightly out of range of Martin's voice, and talked to the other men and the women alike, including the elegant Sharon. She stuck to neither sex and was oblivious of status, concentrating, as was her way, on individuals, regardless of gender. When she was not talking, she was staring intently at Martin.

But mostly she talked. She talked to Ken a long time. She hadn't seen him in years, but he remembered all the details of their relationship. She talked with the others about shopping, language, the media. She was friendly towards everyone. She was in a very friendly mood. She was having a marvelous time.

When it was time to leave, as she got up from the table, Martin called her over.

"Give me a kiss, here and here", he said, pointing to his 2 cheeks. Kiss me in the French way.

Terri obliged. She pecked him briefly and went to pick up her coat in the cloakroom. Ken was in there.

"I hope you enjoy Pakistan "she said, and leaned to kiss him, too."

"Oh come on!" came Martin's voice from outside. "Let's be realistic."

"I used to have some Pakistani friends around here!" Terri cried.

"That's why they're here – because they didn't enjoy Pakistan!" Martin continued, as Sharon tried to shut him up.

He left the pub, accompanied by Sharon. Terri got her coat and left after them, laughing all the way home to Benny Avenue.

He stayed the rest of the night, and in the morning he was gone.

She went to a political meeting at which Martin was being much talked about. People were saying he had become "very defensive" and one person went so far as to say his behavior had become "off the wall."

Terri was upset. She cared for Martin, not only sexually, but in every other way. If he were in such bad shape, it might be partly because of her. If he would only get better she would never further disturb his marital arrangements. He was too valuable for her to destroy him, Whereas she had previously vowed to satisfy her passion, she would now control it for the sake of her beloved's health. It was sad, but she could do that. She must do that.

The next time she saw him, he seemed a bit disturbed, but he was coping. It was at a community event, at which he gave the concluding speech. He had marched into the room and sat in the chair directly in front of her. He did not speak to her. Until he got up to give his speech, he was entirely silent and solemn-faced. He did not stir.

When he spoke he did so eloquently, defending every position he had ever taken in politics up to the present. No one present could deny that he was an influential man. The audience sat in silence. He left the podium and walked out of the room, again silent and with his poker face.

It was a few weeks before Terri saw him again. It was at another meeting and Martin seemed back to his old self. He laughed. He pontificated. He argued. He was no less brilliant, but he did not seem to find it necessary to be on the defensive. He was relaxed. He was happy.

Terri stayed to the end of the meeting. She hoped Martin might give her a drive home. She had to go to the washroom. When she came out, he was gone. Outside, it was raining. She had an umbrella with her, but she discovered it was broken. Still, it would have to do. Drearily, she walked down the steps of the building and out onto the sidewalk, where a car honked behind her. It was Martin.

"Give you a lift?"

"You sure can."

In the front seat was a younger woman (not Sharon) who had also been at the meeting. When introduced, she nodded shyly and smiled, but she did not speak.

"I'm giving Katya a drive home, too."

Martin and Terri started talking up a storm, about the meeting, about their lives in general. He let Katya off first, then Terri at her corner

"Good to see you again, Terri, "he said.

"Good to see you, Martin. Look after yourself."

Terri ran into her building as Martin zoomed off.

This time there was no passionate explosion inside, and she was happy.